BUZZARDS OVERHEAD

Trace Jordan was slowly dying in the saddle from the bullet hole in his hip. The buzzards were already swinging in waiting circles above him. He slid down a canyonside and found a cave under the rock wall. He crawled in and lay down, his rifle pointed at the entrance. But he couldn't keep his eyes open—there was no strength in him.

When he awoke there was a woman kneeling beside him. He felt her cool, deft fingers working at his wound. He watched her, liking the way her hair fell across her shoulders, the swell of her bosom under the thin blouse.

THE BURNING HILLS

BENDIGO SHAFTER
BORDEN CHANTRY
BRIONNE
THE BROKEN GUN
THE BURNING HILLS
THE CALIFORNIOS
CALLAGHEN
CATLOW
CHANCY
THE CHEROKEE TRAIL
COMSTOCK LODE
CONAGHER
CROSSFIRE TRAIL
DARK CANYON
DOWN THE LONG HILLS
THE EMPTY LAND
FAIR BLOWS THE WIND
FALLON
THE FERGUSON RIFLE
THE FIRST FAST DRAW
FLINT
GUNS OF THE TIMBERLANDS
HANGING WOMAN CREEK
THE HAUNTED MESA
HELLER WITH A GUN
THE HIGH GRADERS
HIGH LONESOME
HONDO
HOW THE WEST WAS WON
THE IRON MARSHAL
THE KEY-LOCK MAN
KID RODELO
KILKENNY
KILLOE
KILRONE
KIOWA TRAIL
LAST OF THE BREED
LAST STAND AT PAPAGO WELLS
THE LONESOME GODS
THE MAN CALLED NOON
THE MAN FROM SKIBBEREEN
THE MAN FROM THE BROKEN HILLS
MATAGORDA
MILO TALON
THE MOUNTAIN VALLEY WAR
NORTH TO THE RAILS
OVER ON THE DRY SIDE
PASSIN' THROUGH
THE PROVING TRAIL
THE QUICK AND THE DEAD
RADIGAN
REILLY'S LUCK
THE RIDER OF LOST CREEK
RIVERS WEST
THE SHADOW RIDERS

SHALAKO
SHOWDOWN AT YELLOW BUTTE
SILVER CANYON
SITKA
SON OF A WANTED MAN
TAGGART
THE TALL STRANGER
TO TAME A LAND
TUCKER
UNDER THE SWEETWATER RIM
UTAH BLAINE
THE WALKING DRUM
WESTWARD THE TIDE
WHERE THE LONG GRASS BLOWS

SHORT STORY COLLECTIONS
BOWDRIE
BOWDRIE'S LAW
BUCKSKIN RUN
DUTCHMAN'S FLAT
THE HILLS OF HOMICIDE
LAW OF THE DESERT BORN
NIGHT OVER THE SOLOMONS
THE RIDER OF THE RUBY HILLS
RIDING FOR THE BRAND
THE STRONG SHALL LIVE
THE TRAIL TO CRAZY MAN
WAR PARTY
WEST FROM SINGAPORE
YONDERING

SACKETT TITLES BY LOUIS L'AMOUR
SACKETT'S LAND
TO THE FAR BLUE MOUNTAINS
THE WARRIOR'S PATH
JUBAL SACKETT
RIDE THE RIVER
THE DAYBREAKERS
SACKETT
LANDO
MOJAVE CROSSING
MUSTANG MAN
THE LONELY MEN
GALLOWAY
TREASURE MOUNTAIN
LONELY ON THE MOUNTAIN
RIDE THE DARK TRAIL
THE SACKETT BRAND
THE SKY-LINERS

NONFICTION
FRONTIER
A TRAIL OF MEMORIES:
    The Quotations of Louis L'Amour,
    compiled by Angelique L'Amour

Louis L'Amour
The Burning Hills

BANTAM BOOKS
TORONTO · NEW YORK · LONDON · SYDNEY · AUCKLAND

This edition contains the complete text
of the original hardcover edition.
NOT ONE WORD HAS BEEN OMITTED.

THE BURNING HILLS
A Bantam Book

PRINTING HISTORY

Jason Press edition published May 1956

Bantam edition / August 1956
10 printings through July 1970
New Bantam edition / May 1971
26 printings through May 1988

Photograph of Louis L'Amour
by John Hamilton—Globe Photos, Inc.

ISBN 0-553-24912-6

Published simultaneously in the United States and Canada

Bantam Books are published by Bantam Books, a division of
Bantam Doubleday Dell Publishing Group, Inc. Its trademark,
consisting of the words "Bantam Books" and the portrayal of
a rooster, is Registered in U.S. Patent and Trademark Office
and in other countries. Marca Registrada. Bantam Books,
666 Fifth Avenue, New York, New York 10103.

PRINTED IN THE UNITED STATES OF AMERICA

KR   35 34 33 32 31 30 29 28 27 26

To my Mother—
who also loved the desert

CHAPTER ONE

On a ridge above Texas Flat upon a rock shaped like flame, a hand moved upon the lava. The hand moved and then was still. In all that vast beige-gray silence there was no other movement and no sound.

A buzzard swinging in lazy circles above the serrated ridge had glimpsed that moving hand. Swinging lower, he saw a man who lay among the rocks atop the ridge. He was a long-bodied man in worn boots and jeans, a man with wide shoulders and a lean tough face.

It was the face of a hunter but now of a man hunted. A man who lay with his rifle beside him and who wore a belted gun; but the man still lived and the buzzard could wait.

Below and stretching away from the very foot of the ridge to lose itself in shimmering distance lay the glaring white expanse of the playa. Beyond the playa and even now riding up to draws that would eventually open upon the dry lake were three

1

groups of horsemen who rode with a single thought.

To left and right of the hunted man's position the comb-like ridge stretched away like a great wall dividing the dead white of the playa from the broken lands beyond. Once in those broken lands south of the border, a man might lose himself in any one of a thousand canyons and might himself be lost.

It was a land virtually without water, rarely visited by white men and roved only occasionally by Indians for whom this was a last stronghold and at whose hands no white man could expect mercy.

Great tablelands shouldered against the brassy sky, lofty pinnacles loomed higher still and over all that red and broken land the sun lay hot and dead heat gathered in the sullen canyons.

Far and away, beyond the broken land, some great peaks reached at the clouds, purple with distance, cool, remote and lost. In those mountains there would be water and there would be grass. There a man might find shade; there would be wild game; there would be sanctuary. The hunted man had not turned to look but he knew the mountains were there. He also knew what lay between.

Yet here and there even in that broken desert land between, if one but knew where to look, there would be water.

Northward, not yet within the range of the man's eyes, moved the searching riders. Yet the buzzard had already seen those moving shadows that stirred not with the wind but of their own choice.

The buzzard saw them and after a time saw that these were men.

The buzzard could not reason but he knew the patterns that led to food. His entire life was built upon such fragments of knowledge and he knew that where such groups of men rode, death rode with them.

They were hard men bred of a hard and lonely land, men with eyes red-rimmed from sun-glare, faces whitened by alkali and muscles heavy with weariness. Yet they knew the man for whom they searched could not be far ahead and they pushed on, riding steadily into the hot still afternoon.

Trace Jordan could not see the riding men but he knew they were out there and he knew they looked for him. Once, seven hours ago, they believed they had him and his blood-stained shirt revealed how close a thing it had been.

They had caught him in the rocks above Mocking Bird Pass, brought to bay like a lean and hungry wolf pursued by hounds. And he had fought them there, a lean and hungry man, red-eyed and dangerous, a man driven and battered and hammered but a man not beaten, a man who had never been beaten.

A rifle bullet ricocheting from a rock had ripped an ugly tear through the flesh above his hip and he had lost blood.

They had seen him fall and, not yet knowing the manner of man they fought, they had closed in for the kill. They would be more cautious if the chance came again, for upon the rocks they had left more than blood ... they had left a man dead and another sorely wounded and when finally they closed their trap they found nothing, simply nothing at all.

And then they began to see the fiber of the man they pursued, for he had gone soundlessly from among them, leaving their dead behind. Wounded—for they found his blood upon the rocks—but gone as if he had never been.

Somehow he had stopped the flow of blood; somehow he had left no trail; somehow he had vanished with the desert swallowing him, taking him back as one of her own into the wild loneliness of canyon and playa.

Lean and fierce and lonely, Trace Jordan was a man of wild places and far countries, a man fitted by his experience as a wild horse hunter, cowhand, buffalo hunter and prospector for the task that now lay before him.

His empty canteen rattled upon the rocks when he moved, so he lay still, trying not to think of water, his heart pounding slowly, heavily against the rock upon which he lay. It was time to move ... they would be coming soon. He could not see them but they would seek him out. And he needed rest—rest and water. He must find a place to hide, to wait them out.

Sliding back on his belly until the ridge covered his rising, he got awkwardly to his feet. He swayed then, trying to focus his eyes, gathering his failing strength. He had taken precious time to climb up here, knowing that if his pursuers happened to swing north or south he could gain distance by riding the other way. And time and distance were now the very stuff of life itself.

When he reached his horse he took time to roll a smoke and while his fingers fumbled at the cigarette he considered his problem.

They knew the country and he did not. They would know the trails and the hiding places and moreover they had with them Jacob Lantz, the best tracker in the southwest.

Jordan knew Lantz by reputation, as such men were always known in the west. Tales were told over the campfire by drifting cowhands and retold at bars and gambling tables, the stories of gunmen and trackers, of tough town marshals and crooked gamblers, until the mind of each western man was a storehouse of such information.

Jacob Lantz was a Dutch Indian—his father a Dutch trader, his mother a Ute squaw. Lantz was a man who tracked with his mind as well as with his senses. Even as his eyes spelled out the meaning of a trail, his mind would be probing far ahead to seek out the direction and destination of the man he trailed.

A plan was a dangerous thing, yet a plan he must have, a plan would give direction and purpose to his riding; and as soon as Lantz had time to solve the plan, he must shift to another. Yet there was a chance he might lead them off his trail by such a plan.

First, he would need to point himself toward an obvious destination, a way out of the country. There was a river crossing, one of the few crossings of the Colorado, far to the northwest. That would seem logical to Lantz and to the others, for the trail would avoid towns and people who might pass along information of his passing to his pursuers. So that could seem to be his destination.

Well along the road, he could turn suddenly at some point where his trail would be hard to find and take an entirely different track. Otherwise, knowing the trails, they might find a way to get on ahead and wait for him.

Stepping into the saddle, he walked the horse down the arroyo. Westward the country was a series of towering mesas split by deep canyons. The canyons were easy of access and easy to travel, yet any one of them might prove to be a trap. He might ride for miles to find himself up against a dead end and with no way out.

He must seek out a trail to the top of the mesa. He must ride up where the wind blew and the Indians traveled.

Jordan slumped in the saddle, his body smelling of stale sweat, his clothes stiff with sweat and dust. Under him the horse plodded wearily and Jordan knew the poor beast was drawing on his last reserves of strength. Even that splendid animal, the last of his captured horses, was being defeated by the killing pace and the rough country. And they had been all night and most of the day without water.

A faint deer trail led out of the wash and he took it, leaving the heavy sand for the easier travel of the mountainside.

For an hour he climbed steadily, riding up a long ridge of gravel and sand sparsely dotted with bear grass and prickly pear. Before him the shoulder of a vast escarpment had broken down and among the talus, some of it huge blocks of solid rock, the deer trail led steadily upward toward the mesa top. Riding among the rocks and favoring his wounded side, he turned in the saddle and glanced back.

He was amazed at the distance he had climbed. The comblike ridge lay some miles behind and for a second time he marveled at the good fortune that enabled him to pick out the one pass through that wall.

Trace Jordan assayed his position and found nothing to like. His mind now worked with startling clarity, yet he distrusted it, knowing this clarity was the beginning of delirium. He felt his weakness, knowing he needed rest, water and time to treat his wound.

He needed no one to tell him the caliber of men who followed. Ruthless and relentless, they would never leave the trail until they had left him dead. In knowledge of the country and in numbers the advantage was all theirs.

His trail across the playa would be obvious to any eye but his direction along the wash would puzzle them for a while and every delay was important.

His head throbbed heavily. His mouth was dry, his lips parched and broken. He had a fever . . . he could feel it. His wound would be dirty and he could feel the gnawing agony of it constantly. His hands felt unnaturally large and his head was heavy and awkward.

When his horse crested the mesa at last, he drew

up briefly. He could feel the wind. It was almost cold through his sweat-soaked shirt. He turned in the saddle and looked back again.

Faintly, far away still, a wisp of dust hung against the blue backdrop of the hills. A wisp of dust and then another and still another.

The horse walked on ... the mesa was flat, stretching away to infinity, broken by few rocks and by a scattering of gnarled and twisted cedars and by a few piñon. Sparse grass, tight-clinging to the sand, showed here and there. At places the rock surface of the mesa had been swept clean by the wind. The horse walked on.

He carried a pebble in his mouth to relieve the thirst. Twice he dismounted and walked to relieve the horse of his weight, to let him rest. There was no telling how soon he might again have to make a break for it and the horse's strength might mean his life.

He walked several miles before he fell ...

For a long time he lay where he had fallen, unable to summon the strength to rise. The wind stirred a wisp of hair against his forehead and the horse nuzzled him impatiently. His thoughts no longer clear, he got drunkenly to his knees and got hold of the stirrup, pulling himself erect. Somehow he got into the saddle and, of his own volition, the horse began to walk.

Heat waves shimmered their veil across the distance. A few cottony puffballs of cloud hung against the brassy sky . . . perspiration trickled down his body and weird dust-devils played across the mesa before him. Above the mirage of a distant blue lake the heads of the cedars peered like strange beings from some enchanted world.

He worked his jaws, his brain throbbed heavily and when he shifted his gaze his eyeballs grated dryly in their sockets, moving with painful slowness. There were passages of delirium then, through which were woven thin threads of sanity.

He must rest soon. If he fell now he could not get up again but must lie helpless until his enemies came upon him and killed him. Yet he had done nothing but what any man would have done. He had done nothing he did not have to do.

Old Bob Sutton was dead ... the old bull of the herd shot down in the dusty street, and his sons and nephews would never stop hunting until Trace Jordan had been tracked down and killed.

A few days ago he had been a wild-horse hunter with no troubles. He and Johnny Hendrix had gone broke trying to buck a faro layout and, drifting west, they came upon a herd of wild horses. For a month they lived on the country, finally trapping two dozen horses in a box canyon. One by one they broke them and slapped on their brand, the JH, for Jordan Hendrix. All were good stock, better than they had a right to expect from wild stock. Trace Jordan had gone off to find a market and to buy more grub with their last three dollars, for there were still a few horses they wanted.

A bartender remembered them in Durango and loaned Trace Jordan money for supplies and he returned to camp.

Only there was no camp and there were no horses. All were gone, the camp trampled out by the rush of horses and Johnny lying dead near the water hole with four bullets in him and his gun gone.

The afternoon was still and hot. The sun glared down upon the basin and Johnny lay with his face against the baked earth and two of the bullets in him had been fired into his back while he lay sprawled on the ground. Whoever had done this had wanted to make sure. They wanted to leave nothing behind. Only they hadn't known about Trace Jordan.

There were those back down the trail who knew Trace Jordan as a quiet easy-going man. Hell on wheels with a gun, some said, a man who could follow a trail like an Apache. In the rough-and-tumble brawls of saloon and trail camp he was one of the best. He had killed a man in Tascosa who called him a liar and he killed four Indians who trapped him in a buffalo wallow north of Adobe Walls. And a gun-slinger had died of bad judgment on the Ruidoso. But Trace Jordan was a quiet man.

Slowly, taking infinite pains, he worked out the story of the fight.

Six men had come in from the north. Spotting the horse camp, they had kept back in the brush along the creek and studied the layout.

It must have been about noon. The spilled bucket lay near Johnny and the frying pan lay on the ground near the scattered fire. They had come up, riding slow. Johnny had just filled the bucket and was leaving the spring (his tracks were cut deeper going away from the spring) and he had stopped as they rode up.

Twice in the days that followed Jordan wasted time on streams, yet each time he found the trail again and by that time he could identify the tracks of each of the six horses and those of several of the riders. He had studied their tracks around their camps and around the trails and by that time he knew something of their dispositions and manner of thinking.

One man rarely smoked more than half a cigarette. He occasionally took only a few nervous puffs, then dropped it. Another wore large-roweled Mexican-style spurs that left an imprint when he squatted on his heels.

After a week of such travel he rode into the street of Tokewanna. It was a single dusty street with the usual clapboarded false-front buildings and several of adobe. And a man loitering on the street took one quick, startled glance at the brand on his horse and ducked into a saloon.

Trace Jordan swung down from his horse and loose-tied him at the hitch-rail. Yet when he went into the saloon there was no sign of the man he sought. Trace ordered a drink and looked around at the three men playing cards ... another man leaned against the bar. Trace Jordan glanced at his spurs.

"How about a drink?"

The man moved over as he spoke. He was young, rugged-looking, a working cowhand. When their glasses were filled he lifted his and looked at Trace Jordan. "Here's to you and the trail ahead."

They drank and Trace said quietly, "I may stick around for a while."

"My advice," the young man was smiling, "keep travelin'!"

The implication was obvious. To the man in the street the JH brand on his horse had meant something and that had to mean the man knew about the killing of Johnny. He either knew or had been one of the killers. Obviously, in passing through the saloon he had said something to this man. Trace was now being warned away and that implied the six had friends.

"Had some horses stolen," Jordan said. "My partner was murdered. I trailed 'em here."

The young man was no longer smiling. He took the last drop from his glass and stepped back from the bar. "Depends on how much country a man needs."

Jordan waited the explanation, his eyes missing nothing in the room. The men at the table were alert and listening.

"Six thousand miles out there," the man said, "or six feet here."

The harshness of the trail had drawn him fine. He turned from the bar, a big tough lonely man suddenly showing all the danger that was in him. The young man took a step back, suddenly wary.

"I already bought chips," Jordan said. "They dealt the hand."

He turned from the bar and went through the door and then he saw the big old man coming up the street on the steeldust. Trace had gentled that steeldust himself. He had taken time with the horse. Next to the big red horse he rode, it had been the best of the lot.

The old man had a shock of white hair. His eyes were fierce and commanding. When he stepped down from the saddle there was something of the king in his manner.

Trace Jordan stepped down from the walk and started across the street toward the old man, a tall man with an easy woodsman's walk and the knowledge that he was heading right into trouble. Down the street a man stopped ... another appeared in the entrance to the store.

The brand on the steeldust had been worked over and an excellent job. The JH had been turned into an SB.

The old man looked across the saddle at him, a strong old man with fierce unrelenting eyes. "What's the matter? Lookin' for something?"

Remembering Johnny lying in the dried mud beside the water-hole, Trace told him: "I'm looking for the man who stole that horse from me. He's mine. I caught him. I broke him. I branded him JH."

Quick temper flared in the hard old eyes. "You callin' me a horse thief?" He stepped around the horse to face Jordan. He was wearing a tied-down gun.

"I'm only saying that's my horse you're riding. He's a stolen horse."

"You're a dirty liar!"

When the old man's hand dropped to his gun, Trace Jordan shot him through the stomach.

Jordan looked over the smoking gun at two

bystanders. "Walk out there and lift that saddle skirt, both of you." When they started walking he said, "If there isn't a four-inch white scar under the saddle skirt, I'm a liar."

The scar was there ...

"No matter," one of the men told him, "maybe this is your horse but that old man was no thief. You'd better ride before they hang you."

There was an instant then when Trace Jordan looked down into the dying man's eyes. "That was my horse," he repeated. "My partner was murdered when he was stolen."

All time seemed to stop while the old man struggled to speak but blood frothed at his lips and he died. But of one thing Jordan was sure. The old man had believed him.

From up the street a yell, "He's downed Bob Sutton! He's shot Bob!"

And the doors vomited men into the street.

Trace Jordan hit the leather running and took the big red horse out of town at a dead run. Behind him guns talked but no bullet hit him.

And now he was here, high on a sunlit mesa, dying in the saddle. There was nothing to see but distance, nothing but an infinity of far blue hills and nameless mysterious canyons.

The mustang stopped suddenly, head up.

Jordan turned painfully, searching all around, and in all that vast emptiness there was no living thing to be seen but a solitary buzzard. Heat waves shimmered the outlines of the junipers but nowhere was there movement, nor any sign of life ... and then he saw the tracks.

The tracks of a pack rat in the dust and the tracks of a deer.

They led to the cliff edge and disappeared there. Why did that seem important? His mind fumbled at the puzzle but the mustang tugged impatiently at the bit and Jordan gave the horse his head. The mountain-bred horse swung at once to the cliff-edge and, reaching it, stopped.

Below him was an eyebrow of trail that clung to the cliff face. To this trail led the tracks. Jordan tried to focus his thoughts on the trail. The tracks of a pack rat alone would mean nothing, yet the deer tracks on the same trail could mean water. And the smell of water would have stopped the horse, for the animal must be half-dead with thirst.

Despite his condition he realized at once the possibilities of such a place. His horse, bred to wild country and only a few weeks away from running wild, might take that trail. A wrong step could send them plunging a thousand feet or more to the bottom, yet those tracks might lead to water and a deer had negotiated the trail. And what had he to lose? Going on was impossible ... he spoke to the horse.

Momentarily, ears pricked, the horse hung back, but the urging of the rider and his own promptings decided the matter. The inside stirrup scraped hard on the canyon wall and the outer hung in space but the mustang, walking on delicate feet, went on down the trail, no more than an edge of sloping rock stratum, to a place some forty yards along where the trail widened to ten feet. Here Jordan swung from the saddle and, trailing his

15

reins, he went back up the trail on hands and knees, unable to risk walking in his weakness.

With a handful of bunch grass he brushed out the tracks leading to the cliff-edge and then, taking a handful of dust, he let it trickle from his hand and, caught by the wind, spray over the ground, leaving the earth apparently undisturbed. Then he edged back down the trail and climbed to the saddle.

Concealed from above by the overhang of the cliff, the trail became increasingly dangerous. At one point there was only slanting rock but the big red horse scrambled across while Jordan sat his saddle only dimly aware of what was happening.

Suddenly, after more than a half-mile of trail, it ended in a half-acre of shelf almost entirely overhung by the cliff and entirely invisible from above. The outer edge was skirted by manzanita and juniper that gave no indication from across the canyon of the space that lay behind it. Here, concealed from all directions, was an isolated ledge ... and at one side of the ledge, a ruin.

Without waiting to be guided, the horse walked toward the ruin with quickening footsteps ... and Jordan heard the sound of running water.

Almost falling from his horse, he staggered to the basin where clear cold water trickled from a crack in the rock to fall into a rock basin some dozen feet across. When he had drunk deep of the water he rolled on his back and tried desperately to think.

Wrinkling his brow against the dull throb of pain, he went back over his trail in his mind. Not even Jacob Lantz would find it a simple one. Much of the mesa had been bare rock, nor was there any indication from above of this place he had found. Nor would any man in his right mind attempt the trail to it.

He drank, and drank again, feeling the slow penetration of the cold water through all his thirst-starved tissues. After a time he stumbled to his feet and stripped saddle and bridle from the horse, picketing it on the thick grass.

He would need a fire ... dry sticks that would make no smoke. The ruin would shield the reflection. He must have hot water to bathe his wound. He must ...

A long time later he opened his eyes into darkness. Listening, he could hear no sound but the trickle of water. The night was cold.

Crawling to his saddle, he fumbled at the knots and finally loosened them enough to get at his blanket roll. Wrapping himself in his blankets, he lay still, his head feeling like a great half-empty cask in which his brains seemed to slosh around like water. His lips were cracked by fever ... outside a lone star hung over the rim of a far cliff.

Through the fog of his delirium Jordan listened to the trickle of water. He must be careful ... careful. His enemies might be far away but in the still of a clear desert night, sound carries. And by daylight they would be all around, thirty or forty belted blood-hungry men. And at dawn he must be watching that thread of trail, rifle in hand.

Pain gnawed at his side like a hungry rat ... such a little wound but it needed care, it needed cleansing. His eyes found the lone star above the canyon's rim and held to it and a long time later, he slept. A pack rat appeared at the edge of the trail, peering curiously at the sleeping man, then went on, wary but unfrightened, to the water's edge. Out in the canyon a small stone, long poised by erosion, fell into the depths with a faint, lost sound.

On the mesa's top a long wind stirred, moaning among the junipers and fluttering the campfires of the searching men. A man had been slain and it was the law of their time that the killer must die in turn. A coyote yapped at the moon, a weird cacophony of sound suspended a moment, then scattered by the wind and then the night under the lonely moon was voiceless and still. Only the water trickled and the hunted man moaned softly in his delirium and his sleep.

Through the day-long heat that followed the night, Trace Jordan wavered between delirium and a sick exhausted consciousness. Shortly after daybreak he heard the drum of hoofs overhead and later heard the riders return more slowly. He got his rifle and lay quietly, waiting. If they found him, some of them would die.

He had no animosity for these men other than the six who had killed Johnny. The code by which they operated was his own but it was his nature to fight. There was water here and he had two hundred rounds of ammunition. There was no food, so all he could do was to wait until he starved to death or died of his wound.

He dozed or became unconscious ... vaguely he recalled drinking and bathing his face and his fever-slaked lips. He remembered getting sticks together for a fire to heat water in the bottom of an ancient jar found in the ruins. He removed the bandage to look at the wound. It was ugly and inflamed, frightening to see.

He never succeeded in bathing it. Somewhere along the line of his planning he lost consciousness again ... when he opened his eyes again his head was throbbing, his side a knot of raw pain. He wanted water desperately but was too weak to crawl to it.

The first thing he realized was a sense of movement where no movement should be. He listened, aware of danger, trying to place that faint, mysterious rustling ... *petticoats!* But that was ridiculous.

He felt cool now and comfortable. There was a dull throb in his side but some of the stiffness was gone. His head felt heavy and he did not wish to open his eyes. Something cool touched his brow and he lay still, afraid it would go away. He tried to identify the sounds, fearing he was delirious or dying.

The trickle of water, as always. The horse cropping grass ... a faint wind stirring among the junipers. There was a smell of sage and of wood smoke. This was very close but slight. He kept his eyes shut and tried to place the exact location of his gun. He had no friends within many miles, so anything here, man or animal, was dangerous to him.

The coolness on his brow went away but he felt fingers unbuckling his belt, moving his shirt aside. Fingers cool and deft touched the wound and then

19

something comforting and warm was placed against his side.

He opened his eyes and stared up at the rock overhang. The coolness on his brow was a memory but the pleasant warmth at his side remained. He looked down.

A woman knelt beside him but at first all he could see was a smooth brown shoulder, from which the red blouse had slipped, and a wealth of intensely black hair.

He was delirious ... he had to be. No such woman could be in this lonely place. He was hiding on a wind-hollowed shelf in the face of a cliff, miles from human habitation. And then she turned her head and looked at him.

Her eyes were large and dark, ringed with long lashes, and in that first glimpse he found eyes that were soft with a woman's tenderness ... and then that tenderness was gone and she looked away.

"How you feel?"

She spoke abruptly, her tone giving nothing, neither friendly nor unfriendly.

He tried several times to speak before he could make his lips shape the words. "Good." And then after a pause he indicated the poultice. "Feels good."

She gave no indication that she had heard but arose and went to the edge of the cliff where, concealed by the manzanita, she looked into the canyon. He listened and heard nothing and after a few minutes she returned to his side.

She had built a small fire to heat the water and

now she added some tiny sticks to the little flame. There was no smoke, almost no smell.

"Nice," he whispered. "Nice of you."

She looked around sharply. "I do it for a dog!"

And when she removed the poultice the gentleness was gone from her fingers. He watched her as she worked, liking the way her dark hair fell across her shoulders, the swell of her breasts under the thin blouse. Yet her features were sullen and without warmth.

"If they find you've helped me you'll be in trouble."

"There is always trouble."

There was no strength in him and he lay staring up at the overhang and he must have slept, for when he awakened again she was gone. The fire was cold. His side was freshly bandaged and his face had been bathed, his hands washed.

There was nothing he could do so he was glad no effort was required of him. Yet he could wonder about the girl and it passed the long hours when he lay awake with only remote sounds from the canyon or the distant cry of an eagle. She had been gentle when she believed him unconscious but changed abruptly when she became aware of his attention. It made no sense ... but neither did her presence in this place.

She asked no questions so she must know what he was doing here. She was neat, her clothes not dusty from travel, so she could not have come far to get here. Yet if she lived nearby, the Sutton outfit must know her. Thought of the Suttons made him remember his guns.

Lifting himself on one elbow, he saw his saddle had been brought nearby and his rifle lay against it within reach of his hand. His two pistols in their twin belts, the one he wore and the spare he carried, had been placed near him, their butts within easy grasp.

The opening of the path down the mountain had been barricaded with brush and branches, all dry so the slightest noise among them would awaken him if he slept. Whoever the girl was, she thought of everything and she could be no friend of the Sutton-Bayless outfit.

Yet how had she reached him if the trail was blocked? The thought of another approach worried him and if the girl knew of this place, others must know. For the first time he gave careful attention to the shelf on which he lay.

That part of the hollow exposed to the sun was thick with grass and there were some bushes and trees. Where he lay no sunlight could reach and no rain unless blown by wind. There was grass enough for his horse unless he had to remain too many days. Looking around, he found his tobacco and papers at the edge of the ground sheet upon which his blankets were now spread. He rolled a smoke and when it was alight he lay back, drew deep, then exhaled.

The girl might be an Indian, yet she was no Apache and this was Apache country. Yet neither her facial structure nor manner impressed him as Indian and her inflections were definitely Spanish. Few Mexican families were supposed to live along this section of the border, yet it could be.

It was very hot. He rubbed out his cigarette and eased his position. Sweat trickled down his face. His mouth tasted bad and he dearly wanted a drink, yet lacked the will to rise. Out over the far canyon wall a buzzard wheeled in wide, lazy circles.

No sound disturbed the fading afternoon and across the canyon a great crag gathered the first shadow of evening. Somewhere a horse galloped and then the hoofbeats drummed away into silence and the heat.

Maria Cristina had heard the riders when they first came into the valley. No such group of riders had come to the canyon since her father's death and it would mean nothing but trouble. When as many as a dozen men rode in a group in this country it meant killing.

Turning from the sheep, she walked to the horse that dozed in the shadow of a cottonwood and took from a holster an ancient Walker Colt. Held at her side, it was concealed by the folds of her skirt.

She had no reason to believe the oncoming riders were friendly. She was a Mexican and she owned sheep but aside from that, she was the daughter of Pablo Chavero, who had died up the canyon to the west, fighting even as his blood wrote its epitaph upon the rocks. Listening to the sound of their coming, she could almost see the faces of the riders. Only the Sutton-Bayless outfit could muster so many.

"Juanito! Stay with the sheep!"

Juanito at eleven was already more like her father and not at all like her older brother, Vicente.

She walked away, her hair blowing in the wind, knowing why these men came, and she waited, standing sullen and lonely upon the hillside, expecting nothing.

These would be the same men who had killed her father and driven them to this place. And now if they could find him they would kill the man who lay up there in the rocks, perhaps dying.

It was a vast and lonely land and if her whole family were killed here, there would be none to ask why. Only the restless eyes of the men along the street of Tokewanna would catch fire less often, for she would not be passing, her skirt rustling, her hips moving with the faint suggestion she knew so well how to use.

It had been four years since she had a new dress. Just old things made over. It had been three months since she had been to town to look at the goods in the stores, to finger the cloth she could not buy.

To walk in the town was good. The men stared and made remarks and the women turned away from her, their lips stiff, eyes angry. She was that Mexican girl, "no better than she should be." The women resented her because the men turned to look. Deliberately, she challenged their stares. She might hate them but she was a woman. They despised her but they wanted her too. Among the pale-faced women her dark beauty was an arresting thing. She knew it and liked it so. She knew that the something wild within her was felt by the men. She lifted her chin ... other women had beautiful clothes but she was Maria Cristina.

They came over the crest of the knoll in a tight bunch, then walked their horses down the slope and drew up a dozen yards away. There were ten in the group and all their faces were familiar.

Jack Sutton was the worst of them, recklessly good-looking and a man with death behind him. He looked her over deliberately, insolently, head to foot. "You get better-lookin' every time I see you, Mex! By the Lord, some day I'll—"

"Some day!" Her contempt was a lash. "Some day you get keel!"

Ignoring him, she turned to Ben Hindeman. "What you want?"

There was no nonsense about Hindeman. Shorter than the rangy Sutton, he was a blocky powerful man, his broad jaws always dark with a stubble of beard. "You seen a wounded man on a beat-up red horse?"

"I see nobody. Who come here?"

Sutton was staring at her and she knew he wanted her and deliberately, with every move of her body, she taunted him, hating him both for his contempt and his desire. She was a Mexican and she kept sheep, yet she treated him with contempt and it drove him to fury.

"If you see anybody," Jack Sutton said, "send that kid brother to tell us. Better still . . . I'll come back . . . alone." He looked her over, grinning with no smile in his eyes. "I think you need a man."

She turned her eyes upon him. "Where is a man?" Contempt edged the insult. "*You?*"

Anger whipped his face. "Why, you dirty—!" He leaped his horse at her but, even as the horse sprang, Maria Cristina whipped up the heavy Colt, firing as it lifted.

The blast and flash of the gun made the horse jerk aside his head and almost fall; but a bright spot of red showed on Sutton's ear and blood began to well from it in slow crimson drops.

She held the Colt poised, her expression unchanged. "You go. Next time I no miss."

Unbelieving, Jack Sutton touched his ear and brought his hand away covered with blood. His face was white with shock.

Hindeman's eyes were glinting and he studied Maria Cristina with new attention. "If your horse hadn't shied," he told Sutton, not without an edge of satisfaction, "you'd be dead."

"Why, yes, Ben." Sutton's voice was low. "She would have killed me. That dirty sheepherder would have killed me."

Hindeman turned his horse and the rest followed. Jack Sutton turned in his saddle to look back. "Keep that gun handy. I'll be back."

As they crested the knoll one of the riders lifted his hand in farewell. It was Jacob Lantz.

From a pocket in her skirt she took a cartridge and reloaded the Colt. If Lantz had tracked the man this far there was danger. He was a queer, stoop-shouldered old man, more bloodhound than human. He never bathed and prowled around the hills like a strange cat.

What could the man have done? To make them hunt him so, he must have killed a Sutton. Twice during the morning hours riders paused near the spring and she gathered from talk she overheard that they were working all the canyons with care.

Juanito walked toward her, swinging a stick. "Who do they look for?" he asked.

She looked at him, her eyes warm. When she had turned back from her facing of Sutton she had seen Juanito get up from behind a rock. Only eleven, he was already like her father. He had been large-eyed and pale but he had the rifle.

"A man," she said. "They look for a man."

"I don't want them to find him."

"Maybe they won't," she said.

A rider came down the canyon in worn buckskin breeches and a patched vest. He rode a ragged paint pony. It was her brother Vicente, a tall too-thin young man with a weak face.

She stared at him, feeling no kinship, wondering how a son could be so little like the father. Vicente could draw a gun faster than any man she had ever seen, as fast as Jack Sutton, probably, who had killed eleven men. But Vicente had killed no one, nor was he likely to. He was a weak man, without courage.

"What do they do here?" he demanded. "For whom do they look?"

"You afraid?" she asked contemptuously.

"I am afraid of nothing!" He spoke loudly, glaring at her. "Why should I be afraid?"

"Why? Why, I don't know. Only you afraid. You always afraid of everything."

Juanito could not hold back the story. "Maria Cristina shot Señor Sutton."

Vicente was shocked. "You *shot* him?"

She shrugged. "In the ear, only. His horse jumped."

Vicente stared at her. She would be the death of them all! They had little enough but here they were left unmolested. Why could she not leave well-enough alone? The business of gringos was the business of gringos.

Vicente remembered finding the body of his father. He had worshiped his father and his father had been a strong man and yet for all his bravery and strength they had hunted him down like a crippled wolf and left him dead upon the rocks. What chance then for Vicente?

He stared gloomily at the ridges, wishing they would find the man and go away. Maybe he was a coward. But he was alive and the sun was warm and there was music in the wind.

"I wish they would find him," Vicente said. "Then they would go away."

Maria Cristina stared at him, her eyes black and scornful. "You are a fool."

He started to reply angrily, then rode away, his back stiff with outrage. Did she not know he was the man of the family? To speak so to him! But he could not maintain the outrage for it was she who ran the family affairs and he was afraid of her.

Maria Cristina stared after him but she was already thinking of the other problem. Where could a man hide and not be found by Jacob Lantz?

Yet even if there had been a safer place, to move now was a danger. A man cannot be trailed who leaves no tracks and as long as he could lie quiet on the shelf, he might be safe. But she must be careful ... very careful.

It was Maria Cristina who led her family to this valley after the death of her father. She had learned of the shelf long ago and went there sometimes to be alone. So far as she was aware it was known to no one else. The Indians who once lived there had chosen the site with care. It was not an easy place to find.

She had bought their first sheep, she tended them and saw to their shearing and the sale of the wool. It was she who insisted upon the strong well-built adobe where they now lived. And she had sent to San Francisco for the few furnishings left after her marriage.

She had married a gringo cowhand when she was fifteen and after her father was killed and with him she had gone to Virginia City in Nevada. There he struck it rich in the silver mines and they went to San Francisco, but drink and gambling broke him and he died in a gun battle while drunk. Maria Cristina returned to her family with all the fine pride of her Mexican heritage and the memories of brief days of glory in Virginia City and San Francisco.

When she came the second time to the rock shelf it was suddenly. A rustle of petticoats and a brush of moccasin on a stone and she was there. She had come up some trail from behind the ruin. She knelt beside him in one swift graceful motion, placing a pot on the ground. It was a stew, still hot.

"Eat ... there is no time for talk."

He ate hungrily while she removed the bandage

and examined the wound. It looked little better. She bathed it and replaced the bandage with a clean cloth.

When he had finished the stew she took the pot to the spring and washed it, then returned with a piece of cotton cloth wrapped around some tortillas and some strips of jerked beef. "No fire," she warned, "they look for you."

She started to rise but he caught at her skirt. She looked down at him, her face sullen, revealing nothing.

"Who are you? Where do you come from?" he asked.

"Do I ask this of you?"

"I want to know whom to thank."

"*Por nada.*"

"At least your name."

She said nothing, standing patiently until he released her skirt. She arose with a lithe movement and turned away but he craned his neck to look after her and said suddenly, without conscious thought, "You . . . you're beautiful!"

"I think you talk too much . . . you sleep."

Yet when she reached the ruined wall she stopped. She did not turn her head but when she had stepped over the fallen stones she said, "Maria Cristina," and was gone.

He listened for some further sound of her going but heard nothing but the trickling of the water. She was risking her life to come here. To most of the Sutton-Bayless crowd the fact that she was a woman would mean nothing beside the fact that she was an enemy.

Jacob Lantz was the man he feared. Lantz was a man with a reputation. He had been one of the mountain men, had scouted for the army against the Indians, had hunted and trapped where his will took him. He had lived much with Indians, not only the Utes who were his mother's people but with Navajo and Apache as well. He would watch the girl, knowing she lived nearby and knowing she was an enemy. The wounded man would need food and care and if he was to get it at all, it must be from this family. And Jacob Lantz was not an easy man to outguess.

"Maria Cristina."

He whispered the name, liking the sound of it in his ears. Spanish, certainly. Yet she moved like an Indian and there was about her an innate dignity as typical of the Indian as the Spanish. There was that dignity and a pride of person out of keeping with her surroundings. These things impressed him.

He checked his guns again. There could be no certainty for him. Every moment was a moment of danger. Each hour might be his last. He was leaving no tracks, yet the coming and going of the girl could not long remain unnoticed.

The food he now had was sufficient for a couple of days if he ate sparingly and he knew he must. There was no telling when she could return. Or if she would.

Whatever path she used must be well concealed, yet the fact that his hiding place was known at all worried him. If found, he would have no chance at escape. It was simply a matter of killing until he was himself killed. He could only hope they would come when he was awake.

He lay back, staring up at the rocks. He was very weak and the slightest movement tired him. It must be days, even weeks before he would be fit to travel. And that was long, much too long. Again and again his thoughts reverted to Maria Cristina. A long time ago, in another life, he remembered women who had such poise and bearing. But that had been in the Tidewater region of Virginia when he was a boy.

What could her blood line be? The Conquistadores? Or that even older lineage, of the Toltec kings?

At times he heard riders in the canyon or on the mesa above, so he knew the search continued. And again he watched the evening come, watched the shadows grow long and waited for that lone star above the canyon's rim.

Only tonight there were two. One hung in the sky, the other was lower down, somewhere on the mesa across the way; but this was a fire, the camp-fire of watching men.

CHAPTER TWO

Jacob Lantz was beside that fire and it was seven miles from the ledge on which Trace Jordan lay wounded. Jack Sutton was there with him and a half-dozen others. All were tired and the older men disgusted. The younger ones found it a welcome relief from range work but all were determined. Only Jacob Lantz was tasting the bread of bitterness.

For the first time in years he had lost a trail he could not again find. Jordan had eluded him, either escaping clear out of the country or hiding himself securely.

The trail had simply vanished. Nor was it possible to say exactly where it had vanished. Sutton did not believe Jordan had ever mounted the mesa and Hindeman was inclined to agree. Lantz was positive Jordan had reached the mesa but could not explain why he believed it. He had seen only two fresh tracks atop the mesa and neither could be identified as those of the hunted man.

Jordan had lost blood, much blood. Yet he had kept moving and at no time had he failed to use his head. Such a man was dangerous.

Lantz knew nothing of Jordan but he could read a trail and he knew that Jordan knew wild country and how to cover a trail. And he used none of the obvious methods. Nor had he done the same thing twice.

The country through which they moved was wild and broken. It lay upon the border between New Mexico and Arizona to the north and Sonora and Chihuahua to the south. Water holes were few and the country south of the border was without population for more than fifty miles into Mexico.

In the past there had been bitter fighting along the border but only Pablo Chavero had lasted against the hard-fighting Sutton-Bayless outfit and then he too had gone down. Yet if the hunted man were to get aid from any source it could only be that one family.

"Vicente's yellow," Mort Bayless said.

"That girl isn't," Hindeman said.

"We'd see it if she helped him," Joe Sutton argued. "This country's all wide open."

"Then why don't we see *him?*"

Lantz ignored the conversation, considering the girl. She had no love for any gringo, that much he knew. But most of all she had no love for any Sutton or Bayless. The question was: would she risk all they had by incurring the Sutton anger?

She might ...

He set himself to watch the girl. Vicente, he soon realized, was worried. It showed in the young

Mexican's restlessness and in the way his eyes kept searching the hills. A man of lesser perception might believe he knew something but Lantz surmised the truth. Vicente wanted no trouble and with the Sutton riders in the hills trouble could come at any moment.

Lantz settled himself among the sparse growth above the canyon. He had his glasses with him and he could watch the movement around the house. His was an infinite patience. Neither hours nor days had any meaning when he was on the hunt and his eyes missed nothing.

At dusk he watched Maria Cristina and Juanito bring in the sheep. They were penned near the house, the big dogs were fed and smoke lifted lazily from the chimney.

Vicente came out and chopped wood. Lantz would see the axe rise, then fall and some time later he would hear the sound, mellowed by distance. The setting sun edged the shadows with somber orange as of distant fires blazing. Jacob Lantz lit his pipe and waited. Now would be the time ...

Yet nothing happened. The fingered pinnacles grew tall, the deeper canyons swallowed darkness. Maria Cristina came from the house and he poised like a hound at a vagrant scent but she merely checked the corral bars and returned inside. And then that canyon too was lost in darkness. Only the two visible windows glowed. The night grew cool.

Perhaps he was mistaken. Perhaps they knew nothing. Yet he could go closer at night.

At dusk Trace Jordan rolled from his blankets

and, taking his time, crawled to the edge of the cliff. From behind the screen of brush he looked into the canyon.

For the first time he could appreciate the situation. Below him the canyon was less than a hundred yards wide but within a short distance it spread out into a flat. The canyon was actually a hanging valley that dropped off, some two miles away, into the vast flat that lay on both sides of the border and it was upon that flat where Sutton-Bayless cattle grazed.

In the foreground, almost in the center of the widest part of the canyon lay the Chavero homestead. The canyon at that point was well grassed and along the lower slopes of the canyon where it was not too steep to be grazed he could see the telltale signs of sheep-fat, antelope bush and other plants that were excellent stock feed.

Once his eyes seemed to catch a flicker of movement on the steep canyon side across the way. After watching for a long time he decided he was mistaken.

He lay watching the canyon until the night was wholly dark, unaware that on the opposite slope Lantz was also watching. Feeling a faint chill, he crawled back to his blankets. He lay a long time, sick and exhausted by his efforts, before he could muster the strength to eat a tortilla and a small bit of jerky. He took his time, savoring the food and chewing a long time to make it last.

The girl was taking a great risk and he had no right to permit it, yet he had little choice. Obviously the Suttons believed him in the vicinity or the chase would long ago have gone on. And how long would this hiding place remain unfound? Suppose from the cliff opposite someone glimpsed a darkness where his shelter was? Or detected some chance movement of his?

Maria Cristina was pitting her wits against the cunning of Jacob Lantz and it was unfair

Given an even chance, his brick-dust horse would outrun anything in the country but the canyon was undoubtedly watched and his own strength was not up to a hard ride. He could not stand the pounding of a hard ride over these trails and he had still to find the killers of Johnny Hendrix and to take from them, if possible, the price of his stolen horses.

He was awake with the sun. He ate, then drank deep at the spring. He flexed his muscles, tightening and relaxing them, working his fingers to keep them supple. When the sun came up he moved from the overhang to lie in the warmth and sunlight. Later he started to crawl to the cliff-edge but gave it up. He was too weak.

The big red horse fed on the rich grass at the back part of the ledge. He was invisible unless he got to the edge of the brush along the rim.

The day drew on slowly ...

Whatever Maria Cristina had used in that poultice, it had taken the inflammation from his wound. When he examined it before bathing, he saw it looked much better, although still an ugly gash.

From his saddlebags he got his glasses. They were a strong pair of binoculars purchased at an army post, handy in hunting stray cattle or wild horses. He studied the terrain to know it better, trying to learn the trend of the canyons ... it was well along in the morning when his eyes caught a momentary reflection on the cliff opposite.

Well below his own position, it was high above the sheep. When he had watched the place for a long time he decided his eyes had been mistaken or it had been sunlight reflected from a bit of shale dislodged by some scurrying rabbit or pack rat. There was nothing there . . . and then he saw it again.

It was a scant movement that alerted him. He swung his glasses back over ground previously examined.

The spot seemed to offer no concealment, yet there might be some shallow place in the ground where a man might lie. A man who would be invisible until he moved. And then he saw him, a lean old man with sharp hatchet features, a man who could only be Jacob Lantz.

He lowered his glasses, knowing the danger of looking too directly at a man. Such men had a sharp awareness that warned them when they were watched.

Maria Cristina was with the sheep. The boy was off gathering sticks for the bundle they would take home behind the saddle at night.

Did she know Lantz was on the cliff? Trace tried to think of some way to warn her without at the same time revealing his own presence and it was impossible. He would only wait and trust to the girl's innate good sense.

He tried to judge the distance to where Lantz lay. Four hundred yards? It was across the canyon and down toward the Chavero home ... no, closer to six or seven hundred.

He got his rifle and checked the chamber to see if a shell was ready, then put it aside. He sighted down the rifle barrel first, trying to estimate the drop of the bullet, Shooting downhill could be deceptive. That might come but it must be as a last resort.

Twice Maria Cristina got to her feet. Each time she walked purposefully and each time Lantz moved swiftly along the cliff to keep her in sight. Once she gathered wood, another time it was squaw cabbage for an evening meal. Returning to the shade, she sat there a few minutes, then got up and walked directly to a place under the cliff where Lantz stood but where she would be invisible to the old tracker.

Puzzled, Jordan tried to imagine her purpose. It came to him suddenly. Maria Cristina knew Lantz was watching and was deliberately tormenting him!

There was now no possible way in which he could see what she was doing and to a man of Lantz's mind there could be nothing worse. She might actually be with the hunted man, she might be sending him a signal, she might be hiding food for him.

On the hillside Lantz was restless but the girl sat quietly sewing under the cliff. Yet she had been there only a few minutes when the young man on the paint pony rode up. This, although Jordan did not know, was Vicente.

Vicente drew rein near where Maria Cristina sat and waited for her to speak. When she said nothing, Vicente said, "They are still here."

She made no reply. Maria Cristina loved her brother but his weakness angered her.

"Do you know where he is?"

"Who? Of whom do you speak?"

"The man they seek. This Jordan."

"What do I know? Until now I did not even know his name."

Vicente stared uneasily at his sister. She was simple like Rosa, his Navajo wife. He understood Rosa, he also understood his mother. This one was different. Perhaps it was because she had married that gringo and gone away to live in cities ... but no, she had always been a strange one.

She would walk out with no man, yet when she went to town she swished her skirts at them. This was not good. Sometime he would have to kill somebody over her. Why did she not take a man like other women? A woman without a man was nobody.

And she knew something about the man they hunted. The knowledge frightened him. If Jack Sutton or Ben Hindeman found they had been helping the wounded man, they would kill all of them, every one. Or they would kill Maria Cristina.

If they tried that, he, Vicente, must fight. And he did not want to fight. He was only one man and there were many of the others.

Maria Cristina knew what her brother was thinking. She even knew what Jacob Lantz was thinking and she had known since early morning that he was on the hillside. She had known he would be there and, knowing all this canyon, she soon knew exactly where he was. It was not a problem yet. The man up there had food and there was water. If necessary he could manage at least two days alone.

When she had first come upon him she believed him dead. Had she left him alone then, he would now be dead and no problem at all. And he was a gringo.

This stranger was nothing to her. She had no liking for any North American. Only her husband ... he had been kind, even when drunk. Always a gentleman, too. Even now, remembering all his weakness, she had a queer respect for him.

That one up there ... he was not weak. Nor was he soft. She remembered his guns. They were cared for. His jeans were polished where the holster chafed ... this was a man who had lived with a gun.

She turned her thoughts from him. He would be all right, that one. When his strength returned he could ride. That would be an end of him ... and good riddance.

Vicente was restless. He sat the worn saddle and rolled a cigarette. He liked the sunlight on his back. He did not know they were watched but knew they must be. He drew deep on the cigarette and Maria Cristina looked up at him. There was only that to

be said for him. The way he sat a horse and wore
a gun.

"I think you too much frighten, Vicente. You ...
who are good with a gun. I think you better than
Jack Sutton."

Vicente was so astonished that he rode away. It
was the first time Maria Cristina had said one
word of praise to him. But better than Jack Sutton?
No . . . no, it could not be. Yet the thought remained. She believed he could do it.

All that night and the day following Trace Jordan lay quiet and rested. He nibbled at his food,
drank a lot and slept. His thoughts reverted to
Maria Cristina. There was a kind of strong fierce
pride about her that got into a man's blood, no
matter how sullen she might seem.

At dusk three riders appeared on the crest, out
of the canyon below. Lantz slipped out of his hiding place on some signal and went to meet them.
Jordan watched, but without the glasses, for the
sunlight was shining into the shelf and he was
afraid a reflection, even from behind the brush,
might warn of his presence.

The sheep were starting home. He looked again
quickly. Maria Cristina was not with them!

Lantz finished his talk with the men and started
back. Jordan reached for his Winchester, an automatic gesture. Yet almost at the point where Lantz
could have seen the boy was alone with the sheep,
he turned back for a final word.

A stone rattled and Jordan turned swiftly. Maria
Cristina had come around the ruined wall. Her

breath was coming fast, her eyes were wide. She had a small package of food. She turned to go and he caught her hand. "*Cuidado!*" He indicated the riders. "Hurry! They will find you gone!"

Her eyes held his, cold, inscrutable. "You are afraid they will find you? Or that you will get no more food?"

"Don't be a fool," he said shortly.

She turned abruptly away.

"And be careful," he said. "You are a beautiful woman, Maria Cristina."

She looked at him, her eyes flaring a little, yet as she seemed about to speak she suddenly turned away.

Lantz had disappeared and the other riders were riding away when he looked around. Rifle in hand, he moved to the cliff-edge. He had no doubt of what he would do if Lantz saw the girl and followed her. He could kill him.

That night, long after darkness had come, he got to his feet for the first time. Using his rifle as a crutch, he took two steps, then had to sit down. Later he managed two more.

The sheep were penned and Juanito was inside when Maria Cristina approached the house. She circled to come up from the spring where she had left a bucket. She could hear angry voices within the house. One was Vicente. His eyes were flushed and angry when she came into the house.

Her mother shot a quick glance at Maria Cristina from dark, worried eyes. Maria Cristina had en-

tered in the midst of a quarrel gone suddenly
silent.

Vicente stared at her in sullen anger. Head high,
she crossed the room to wash her hands. Her mother began placing food upon the table. Juanito sat at
the table, holding his knife; the room was lighted
by candles and by the fire. It was a large room, a
living-room as well as a kitchen. There were three
bedrooms and a parlor, never used.

Vicente paced the floor. Suddenly he turned on
her. "You'll get us all in trouble! Hiding that man!"

Maria Cristina looked at him, her eyes disdain-
ful. "You are a fool," she said.

He glared at her, furious. He started to speak,
then plunged through the door and slammed it
behind him. Maria Cristina looked after him, her
lips tightening. Feeling as he did, there was no
telling what he might do. Yet he did not know of
the hiding place on the cliff. Not even Juanito
knew.

And he was right, of course. It was a danger to
them all to help the wounded man. Yet she had
found him alone, wounded and dying, and it had
seemed there was nothing else to do.

Vicente stomped back into the house and,
seating himself, began angrily to eat. "You have no
right," he said. "Where is he?"

"I don' know what you talk about."

Vicente half-sprang to his feet. "You know!" he
shouted. "You hide that man! You feed him!"

"And if I do?"

"They'll burn us out! They'll kill the sheep!"

"And what would you do? Fight or run?"

Vicente glared. "I would fight!"

"All right . . . I fight now."

Sullenly he returned to his eating and when he had finished his meal he got to his feet and went outside. He paused by the window and Maria Cristina looked at him, a tall young man, too thin, in worn and shabby clothes. She felt a sharp pang . . . it was not right . . . Vicente had no youth. No bright time of riding, no colorful clothes and the courting of girls. He had grown up a frightened and lonely boy in a land of strangers. It was no wonder he had become a frightened young man.

Vicente was right. She should not bring trouble to her family. They had been born to trouble and had lived always in the shadow of fear. She, at least, had the few good years away from here, even if there had been bitterness in those years also.

Why should she help the man on the cliff? Because he was the enemy of her father's killers? She had not given it a thought at the time. Because he had been hurt . . . ?

She had listened to his delirious muttering and he had called upon no woman. Why should that be important?

Yet there was something quiet and sure about him, something that brought her peace, even in the midst of trouble, something that stilled her restlessness. The memory of it disturbed her so she brushed away the thought. Her imagination, that was all. She was no longer a child to be excited by any drifting cowpuncher.

Trace Jordan got to his feet in the darkness and tried using the rifle for a crutch again. He moved carefully. Tonight a rolling pebble might be heard for some distance and he dared make no unusual sound. Yet he belted on his gun and tried it, knowing his hands would need their skill. He would need his guns. At any minute they might come.

· Considering that, he went around the ruin to the way up used by Maria Cristina. It was a steep slide of talus in a wide crack in the rock wall but as she had made no sound ... he saw it then, a narrow ledge, only inches wide, along the edge of the rock slide.

He returned to the spring and drank deep and long. He never seemed to get enough water. A gentle wind stirred and he caught a whiff of wood smoke. They were still out there, just across the canyon, waiting for him to make a mistake. Had they a clue? Or was it the intuition of old Jacob Lantz?

Despite his weakness he was restless and the big red horse was uneasy too. The grass was growing short now and the horse could not be fed for many more days. They had been penned too long, yet to try an escape now was out of the question. Using the rifle as a crutch, he kept trying his muscles. He knew only that when the time came it would be suddenly ... he was always hungry now. Was it a sign of recovery?

He had begun a systematic study of the country. Knowing desert lands, he could sort out the canyons and ridges and make sense of a sort. Even canyons have a pattern . . . the thought of attempting that trail up the cliff face at night made him sick to the stomach but by day they would be an open target, pinned to the cliff's face.

What of Maria Cristina? So lonely, so sullen, so remote? She was proud . . . it showed in every line of her body, every move. Her clothes might be shabby but her manner was that of a queen.

Yet he had no right to think of her. He must think only of getting away for his every minute here was a danger to them all. He moved suddenly and the movement brought a gasp of pain that doubled him over. He sank to his knees, fighting for breath. If one unexpected movement could do that to him escape was impossible.

He crept back to his blankets and slept and then a long time later he awakened with a start. His hand dropped over the butt of his gun . . . what had awakened him? No ordinary sound in the night would have done it, his subconscious was too familiar with such sounds. It would have to be some other sound, something that did not belong to the quiet symphony of the night.

Wind stirred, a faint breeze. The night was wide, white and still. The pinnacles gave birth to long shadows . . . he had been mistaken then. It had been imagination or fever. Yet he stood a moment longer. The air he drew into his lungs was fresh and cool as mountain water and the stars hung like lanterns in the sky. He knew the feelings, the smells. He knew the long hours of heat, the moving cloud shadows, the thousand canyons with their thousand untold stories. He knew the tumbledown pueblos and the kivas and the mysterious trails left by the Old Ones and marked by their rock piles ... there were rock piles beside the trails in Tibet, he had heard ... his side was itching tonight. Maybe the flesh was beginning to heal.

He turned back, then stopped abruptly. He heard a faint sound, something moving down below in the canyon. He listened ... the bright moonlit stillness brought tiny sounds to his ears. Barely audible. Something ... somebody was moving down below.

Breathless he held himself, aware that somebody or something could hear also. And might already have heard him.

Had he made a sound in his delirium? He did not believe so, for a man's subconscious remains on guard always. Yet the rock walls were like sounding boards and he could hear easier what moved below than they could hear him.

He heard the faint stirring again ... had the searcher some clue? He could not be looking for tracks at this hour, yet ... ? The night was empty again. Far off a plaintive coyote begged the sky.

"It ain't no way reasonable." Joe Sutton stared irritably into the fire. "No man drops out o' sight the way he done."

Ben Hindeman rolled his tobacco in his jaws, not talking. He was reasoning it out in his slow, methodical way. Of them all, Hindeman was the only one to whom Jack Sutton ever took a back seat and Joe had his own ideas about that. Jack, for all his gun-slinging, was a little afraid of his hard-jawed brother-in-law.

"Lost him," Mort Bayless said, "over on that mesa and he was in bad shape. He didn't get far."

It was Mort's brother whom Jordan had killed at Mocking Bird Pass and Mort had been one of them with Jack at the killing of Johnny Hendrix. He had no particular worry about Jordan ever getting him ... he wanted to get Jordan to even up for his brother and because he was a killer by nature.

"If he ever got to the mesa at all," Joe said.

During the last two days the search had dwindled away and Jack Sutton was pleased. Two of the boys had returned to cut hay, another had a wife who was expecting. The need for many men was past and as he fingered the thick scab on his ear lobe, he wished they would all go home. He had plans of his own and the capture or killing of Trace Jordan had become secondary.

Ben was the one he wanted to go back. Ben didn't want the Mexicans bothered and had it been anyone but Ben he would have believed him soft on the girl. But not Ben. He was never soft on anyone. That very lack of feeling made Jack uneasy. Ben was tough and in his slow way he was smart.

Jacob Lantz leaned over and filled his cup with coffee. "He's around," he said flatly.

Ben's head came up. "You see him?"

"No ... but he's here."

"How d' you know if you ain't seen him?" Jack demanded irritably. Sometimes Lantz's cocksureness infuriated him.

"If Jake says he's here," Hindeman said, "then he's here."

"I don't know why," Lantz said, "but I feel it."

"If he's here," Mort Bayless poked the fire, "them greasers know it. I say we just ride down there and take that girl—"

"We'll do nothing of the kind." Hindeman did not even look around.

"She wouldn't talk, no way," Lantz said.

"I'd make her talk!" Mort said savagely. "You'd see!"

"You're a fool," Hindeman said. "You could kill her and she wouldn't talk. Not that one."

Lantz took his coffee and a dish of beans to one side. Meanwhile his ferreting mind gnawed at the problem. A wounded man, alone ...

"Got to be close," Hindeman said. "If he's alive he's eatin' and if he's eatin' he's gettin' it from the Mexicans. But Vicente is the only one ever leaves the place."

Jack Sutton was stretched on a blanket. He lifted himself to an elbow. "Mort, tomorrow you an' Joe stick to Vicente. Go where he goes. Stick tight to him."

"Won't get us nothing. I think it's the girl."

"Jack's got the idea, Mort. Stick to him. He'll break. He'll make a wrong move or he'll talk." He turned his leonine head. "Don't crowd him, just watch him."

Lantz was beginning to know Jordan. He was a man who had been up the creek and over the mountain ... when they caught him it was not going to be fun.

"I'll find him," he said. "When I find him, you boys can have him."

They looked at him, this wry old man with his sour-smelling body and the look of secret humor about him.

"What's that mean?"

"Some of you boys won't ride back. This one's a curly wolf."

Somebody snorted his disgust and Mort Bayless turned impatiently. Jack Sutton was angered by Lantz's attitude, yet he was well aware that without him they wouldn't have come this far. Old Bob Sutton had kept Lantz around and now it was Ben.

Jacob Lantz went to his blankets and rolled up. Staring morosely at the sky, his thoughts ran back over the terrain. There had to be a place and it had to be close by.

Morning was a suggestion of pale light when Jordan awakened. His first thought was of the creeping sounds of the previous night. He must be very careful.

By daylight he examined the steep chimney of talus. A girl or a child might manage that narrow ledge but one wrong step ... that girl was one to mother a race of warriors. Yet a man might slide a horse down the incline of talus. He had seen wild horses do stunts almost as dangerous. Yet a man might wind up at the bottom with a broken leg and have to shoot it out.

Jordan saw the young man he took to be Maria Cristina's brother start up the canyon on the paint pony. As he rounded a bend in the canyon, two horsemen fell in behind him. Twice the young Mexican turned to look back.

Two more riders rode up to the house and dismounted near the stable. So it had gone that far. Every move of the Chaveros was to be watched. Another man came out of the willows and walked toward Maria Cristina. She saw him coming and waited, her black hair blowing in the wind, her skirt stirring. She stood very straight.

Several minutes they talked. Her manner was cool and imperious. There was something fascinating in her face as he watched through the glasses, something proud and fierce that sent a strong eagerness through him.

The man to whom she talked was Jacob Lantz, a man without emotion, a man with an obsession. Whatever he said left her unstirred and when she moved her dress clung to her hips and thighs. He put the glasses down and mopped his face. It was going to be a hot day.

No question about it. He would have to go. He had no right to cause more trouble. He would make a break for it. Returning to his blankets, he settled down to wait for darkness.

Awakening with a start, he found it was already night and he heard a faint rustle of sound. He came swiftly to his feet, gun in hand. Then, holstering the gun, he moved swiftly to the ruin. Drawing back against the wall until the shadows folded him into their darkness, he waited ...

At first, no sound but the trickle of water; then a faint whisper of movement, a suggestion in the night, a sound of breathing ... his hands went out, grasping for a throat.

His hands caught at flesh ... there was an instant of fierce struggle ending abruptly when his hands found the soft contours of a woman's body. "Maria Cristina?"

"Let me go."

The voice was cool, almost detached. Yet there was tension in the body he held. Reluctantly his hands relaxed their hold but he did not move them away.

She stepped back, letting his hands fall. He could hear the sound of her breathing. A little faster from the climb? From the struggle? Or ... ?

"Thought it was Lantz."

She did not reply. There was a suggestion of perfume, some flower scent, faint but clinging. He could see the outline of her face against the outer sky. "I'm going," he said. "I'm getting you all into trouble."

Still she did not speak nor move. The lone star hung above the canyon's rim. "If you had not come along, I'd be dead."

Her face turned toward him but it was all darkness and he could see nothing of her expression.

"You're a woman who could walk beside a man, Maria Cristina. Not behind him."

"You talk too much."

"Maybe ... maybe not enough."

Trace Jordan searched for words but found none. There was a time he had talked easily to women but with this girl and at this time he could find no words for what was within him.

A quail called questioningly into the night and there was no reply. He smelled again the smoke from the watchfires of the hunting men and heard the wind stirring the manzanita, yet he was only faintly aware of them, so conscious was he of the nearness of Maria Cristina.

"You must not go."

"Got to . . . they know I'm close by."

Again she was silent and he did not understand her silence. He walked to the horse and picked up the bridle so suddenly that the horse shied violently. He waited until the horse quieted, then saddled up.

The mere act of swinging the saddle to the animal's back took his wind and caught at his wounded side. He leaned against the horse to catch his breath. Bleakly he stared across the saddle into the night. If he got out of this alive he would be pulling more than his proper share of luck.

"You cannot go up."

"The slide?"

"It is best but there will be much noise."

He tightened the cinch. She had accepted his going then. Glad to be rid of him, most likely. Yet he felt a curious reluctance to go. He remembered the feel of her body, tense and fighting for that moment she was in his arms. The memory brought blood rushing to his head and he turned suddenly and reached for her in the night.

She started to step back but his arms were around her. She fought fiercely, with almost tigerish wickedness yet he held her and drew her close. Suddenly then, she relaxed but it was no submission. She remained still in his arms but there was no response, none whatever. When he released her she made no effort to move away.

"I think you are animal."

Her voice was low, without emotion. He took her in his arms again, kissing her gently this time, kissing her lips and cheeks, her neck and shoulders. She did not respond but neither did she move away. He released her again and stepped back, his breath slow-drawn. And then for a time neither of them spoke. She made no attempt to leave but neither did she invite any further advances.

He felt strangely lost, helpless. He wanted to reach her, to get beneath the surface. Yet there was nothing from her, simply nothing at all.

"You go home," he said. "I'm leaving tonight."

She stooped and picked up the package she had dropped. "Here is food." She seemed to hesitate an instant, then turned away.

"Maria Cristina?"

She stopped but did not turn around.

"I'm coming back."

She seemed not to have heard him. "Ride up the canyon. Take the first wide canyon to the left. Cross the mesa top to the next canyon, then cross that canyon and the second mesa. You will see a red rock like a steeple and there will be a dead cottonwood at its base. Behind the steeple rock there is a place to hide, and there is a way to escape into the desert when the time is right."

"Join me there."

She seemed to shrug. "For why I join you? You think I am gringo? I am Mexican."

"You come, Maria Cristina. I want you."

"You are a fool."

He walked up behind her and she half-turned her head toward him. He could see her face in the vague starlight and the dark pools of her eyes.

"I'm coming back. I owe you more than I can pay."

"*Por nada.*"

"If you do not come to the steeple rock, I shall come back for you."

"You be keel."

"So . . . but I'll come back."

He started to take her in his arms but she stepped back, her eyes flashing. "What you think? That I am some common woman to come when you call? Some woman you take when you want? I am not. You think I come here because I need a man? I need no man. I come because you die here . . . and my father die on those rocks down there. You take me for cheap woman. You go."

He waited quietly until she was through and then he said, "I'm coming back for you, Maria Cristina."

"You are a fool."

"Know more about horses than women," he admitted. "And you're all mustang."

A coyote voiced a shrill rumor to the sky and listened to his own echo. Waited, then tried again. The lone star hung on the canyon's rim like a lost lantern.

"Man once said there were in a man's life certain ultimate things and just one ultimate woman. You're that woman for me."

"No."

He took her gently by the shoulders and kissed her lightly. "You just ain't halter-broke, that's all. I'll be back."

She walked away from him then, without turning, and he heard her start down the slide. If they heard her coming and were waiting, then he knew what he would do. He would go down shooting ... and he would go fast.

Trace Jordan waited until he was sure Maria Cristina had cleared the narrow part of the canyon and was in the meadow near the corral. Then he led the horse to the lip of the slide.

The horse might break a leg or be otherwise injured but it was a chance he had to take. He was through here and he knew they would stay close until he starved or somebody lost their nerve and talked.

He knew how small was his chance. There was not one possibility in a million of getting down that slide unheard. And there were two men up the canyon who would be waiting for him.

He was in no shape for a hard ride. But men in just as bad shape had come through. And there was no other solution. He checked all his gear. His bed was rolled, his canteen filled. The food packet was shoved into a saddlebag. He was wearing both guns now and the rifle was in the boot.

He was stalling ... he knew he was stalling. The thought of tackling that steep slide in the darkness made his mouth dry and his stomach hollow. He gathered up the reins, then stood listening.

There was no sound . . . were they down there in the darkness now, waiting for him? Had they captured Maria Cristina?

Lantz shook Ben Hindeman's shoulder. The fire was low and nobody else stirred. It was very late and the coyote had suddenly stopped his howling.

"Ben . . . wake up."

Hindeman's eyes opened and he was instantly awake. He turned his head a little, listening. He heard no sound but the old tracker was bent over him. "What is it, Jake?"

"We got him, Ben. We got him right where we want him."

Hindeman sat up and began drawing on his boots. His mouth was tasting frightful and his head felt heavy. His eyes told him what time it was after a glance at the stars. He felt sticky and unpleasant but it was time this was finished off. It had taken too much time already.

"The girl's been gettin' to him. Shelf up on the rock wall, must be quite a bit of space up there because he's got his horse up there with him. He'll be comin' down tonight, I think."

"How'd you figure that?"

"Hunch."

Lantz sat back, thinking about that. "More'n a hunch," he said. "Girl packed him a big bait of grub. Long time up there. I don't know how she gets there or where the place is, exactly, but I know where he'll show."

Hindeman got up, stamping into his boots. Then he spoke sharply and heads lifted. At his orders they began quickly to dress. There was some low grumbling, none of it serious. Just the automatic grumbling of tired men awakened from a quiet sleep. Yet all were glad to be called. They wanted it to be over with. The hunt had begun in a burst of passion. With most of them that was gone now and the hunt continued out of duty and their natural reluctance to admit themselves defeated.

"The two men up the canyon," Lantz said. "I woke them up. If he comes that way, they'll take him. There's two men down canyon below the Mexicans' place. He's in the bottle and we've got the thing stoppered."

Jack Sutton pulled on his boots and stood up. He was unshaved and his jaws itched under the stubble. He felt unbathed and dirty and he was a man who liked to be clean.

So the girl had known after all? How many times had she been up there with him?

"That—!" The words broke from him, emptying some of the rankling bitterness within him.

Lantz did not look around and Ben Hindeman merely picked up his saddle and started toward the picketed horses. The other men were belting on guns or picking up their rifles and walking into the night.

They moved out in a tight bunch, then divided. Jack Sutton went along with Ben Hindeman. Once the rest of them were gone, he'd take care of that girl. As for Jordan ... Sutton felt a tightness in his throat ... an ugly feeling.

Trace Jordan held up a moment longer on the edge of the slide. He felt the red horse put out a tentative hoof, then draw back. "Come on, Jed!" He stepped into the leather as he spoke and felt the horse lurch forward, rocks sliding under his feet.

The horse scrambled, slipped and fought for footing. They were going down fast but so far the red horse was taking it well. He was taking enormous forward leaps when Jordan heard the shot.

The harsh bark of a heavy pistol . . . then a second shot, both fired from near the house. Then, above the echoes of the shots and the falling of rock, he heard the high ringing cry. It was no cry of fear or pain but one filled with reassurance and hope.

She had fired to draw their attention from him, so they must be alerted and ready.

He plunged down the last few feet of the slide, the horse scrambling beneath him, and then they were at the bottom and the big red horse moved out, running on the hard-packed sand and running free.

Jacob Lantz heard the rocks of the slide. He swore softly, remembering the looks of it. A man who would come down that in the night—!

"Come on, Ben," he said. "He can only go up or down the canyon. We've got him."

CHAPTER THREE

Ahead of him the shoulder of the canyon bulked black against the sky. It was near here he had seen the two riders earlier in the day. He slowed his horse, making only a small sound on the sand. There was a low mutter of voices, a shadow that moved. He slammed home the spurs and the startled horse gave a convulsive leap forward and broke into a gallop.

A startled curse, a man who lunged and shouted, a gun blasting off to his right and then his own gun smashed sound into the stone corridor and sent a racketing of sound off down the limestone cliffs.

He had fired point-blank at a moving spot of darkness and then he was away, his horse running up the canyon at breakneck speed. Behind him were other shots and shouts ...

Deliberately he slowed his pace. Behind him he heard a rush of horses, startled shouts and replies. On his left a canyon mouth opened, almost choked with brush, but the horse found an opening. Brush slapped at his face and clothing as he pushed through.

High up the rock wall moonlight glanced off the rocky trail. Trees left a space for a rider and he forced a way through, finding the vague trail that led up the cliff. Ten minutes later he was white in the moonlight atop the mesa, yet already they were behind him and he heard hoofs click on the lower trail.

Swiftly he glanced around. Poised on the rim was a rock as large as a piano. He swung down and got behind it, trying its weight with his hands.

Below there was movement. He stooped, took the strain, paused to gather strength, then heaved. The rock tipped, grated, then hung. Overhead was the moon, his body smelled of sweat and dust, his boot toes gripped the mesa top ... the rock tipped, grated, leaned further out. Alone on the mesa's rim he stood, the veins swelling in his brow, throbbing in his throat. Suddenly there was a stabbing pain in his side and then the rock fell free.

He went to his knees, gasping, his mouth wide, feeling the blood inside his pants, perspiration dripping from his brow.

The boulder tumbled off into the vast blackness below, there was a rattle of accompanying gravel, an agonized cry of animal fear, a wild scramble and then the forlorn screams of a horse and a man falling away into darkness. A splintering crash then, a brief chatter of small stones following ... and silence.

Alone on the cliff's edge, his chest heaving with effort, he suddenly filled with some primeval berserk fury and he shouted, his voice rolling down the corridor of rock, "Come on, damn you!"

Sweating and trembling, his body shaken with pain, he leaned a moment against the saddle, gathering strength. They would think awhile before they tried that path again this night. He remembered the lost lonely cry of the man falling off into space and death. *He asked for it,* he told himself. *They stole our horses, they killed my partner and they want to kill me.*

He wanted to live ... the night was cool and still as only a desert night can be ... he wanted to live ... and in his mind there was a memory of the feel of a woman's body, the memory of her lips, of her silent waiting, not fighting, not denying, not accepting. Just waiting.

Over a mesa white in the moonlight he rode steadily, his torn side a throb of agony, and he rode until the sun was rising, until it seemed he had never known any other life than the saddle, never anything but pain, never anything but flight.

Before him in the gray light was a dull red finger of rock and at its base, an ancient cottonwood, white-limbed and dead. He pushed his horse through a curtain of willows into a pocket of rock and trees almost encircled by a tiny stream. The aspen were gray with morning, the grass dew-wet and heavy when he drew rein at last. An old rock house crouched like a tired hound against the cliff's face and there he slid from his saddle and drank.

For a long time then he lay still until the morning sun warmed his shoulders and crept along his tired muscles and ate away the night's chill. He made coffee, ate of the beef and tortillas and then he slept.

At first, when he awakened, he listened for a long time. Birds chirped and played among the branches, his horse cropped grass, the stream chuckled over its stones. Only when he was sure he was alone did he rise and strip off his shirt.

His wound had been torn open by lifting the rock but he bathed it, then bandaged it again with the same cloth. Then from near the steeple rock he studied the trail down which he had come and moved out to brush away the last few tracks. Most of the trail was over bare rock and, although there would be signs, there would not be many.

Every hour of delay was an hour's gain. Would they be so anxious to pursue him they would not bother Maria Cristina? There was hope of that. In any event, he could do nothing. Yet the men who had shot into the back of a dying man would stop at nothing. They had started after him to avenge Bob Sutton's death but now another man had died and, recalling the cry from the canyon ... perhaps two.

Trace Jordan searched for and found a way out of the hiding place. He found it late in the afternoon, a trail screened by brush that led over the rocks and away to the south. He was, he knew, either in Mexico now or close to the border. The way north was barred to him, the way south lay through Apache country. Yet it was the only way that remained.

The killers of Johnny Hendrix were among the

pursuers, yet there were honest cowmen there, too. He wanted his horses back and he wanted the killers to pay, yet if he stayed there would be no end to the killing. Johnny was dead but the Sutton-Bayless outfit had lost several men. It was price enough.

And there was Maria Cristina. ...

He had his first hot meal in days over a fire of dry curl-leaf, almost smokeless, back in the rocks. Yet he was restless. There was no telling what they might do to a girl alone. She had a brother but one man would be helpless against that crowd. He rolled a smoke and settled back. There was no sound of pursuit ... nothing.

Below him the stream gulped and fussed among the rocks, a bird fluttered his plumage. Then far up the canyon, a hoof struck stone.

Trace Jordan came soundlessly to his feet and took up his rifle. He crossed the rocks to a position where he could see the trail. And then for a long time the night was still.

Vicente was at the table when Maria Cristina came from her room. Surprised to find him around so early, she went past him to the fire. Coffee water was on and she added coffee.

Vicente looked up from the table. "Do not take the sheep out."

She turned to look at him. His face seemed older in the morning light, quieter than she had ever remembered it.

"I will take them," he said.

"You?" She was astonished.

"They must be saved."

She stood up then and faced him. The sun was not yet up and the two were alone in the room. For the first time she saw the rifle by his chair and he wore an extra cartridge belt ... it had been her father's belt. "You think they will come here?"

"They will come," he said.

She turned from him and broke an egg into the pan, trying to order her thoughts. Vicente was different. He was a man. She looked at him, puzzled by this change in a brother she now felt she had never understood.

"I will take the sheep to the Notch," he said. "They will not look for them there."

This, then, was what Vicente had sought to avoid. Now that it had come he was no longer afraid. Shame filled her. Shame that she had doubted him, shame that hers had been the fault.

There was quiet resolution in his narrow face and she realized at last that he had never been afraid, only he had sought to avoid an issue that could only result in defeat and destruction for the Chaveros.

"Vicente ..." It was as near as she ever came to a plea for understanding. "He is a good man. I could not let him die."

He took the eggs from the pan, a tortilla from the warm pile on the plate. "It is enough that you have a man."

She returned to the fire, humbled by his quiet dignity. He would take the sheep to the Notch. It was, of course, the best place for them. The Sutton riders did not like sheep but out of sight might also be out of mind. The Chaveros could build another house but the sheep were all they had.

"Take the others with you," she said.

"And you?"

"It is I they will want. If I am not here they will follow."

"You are my sister. I will stay."

"Go . . . I can handle them."

Vicente hesitated. The others would need him. Juanito was too young and without Maria Cristina or himself his mother would be helpless. And his wife, Rosa . . . she was a fine girl but she did not plan.

Maria Cristina had handled men before. This time she might succeed where his presence might precipitate violence.

The sun was not yet up when she saw them go. Juanito started ahead with the sheep, then her mother and Rosa with the burros, loaded with some useful, some foolish things. Vicente held his rifle in the hollow of his arm and this morning for the first time he had tied down his holster. He stood very straight this morning and his eyes were proud. Yet he was quiet at the end. "When you can . . . come."

"I will, Vicente."

Dry-eyed, they stared at each other, this brother whom she had despised and loved, now no longer to be despised. There had never been emotion between them; there could be none now.

"Vicente . . . go with God."

He turned his back abruptly and caught the pommel. An instant he remained so, his back full upon her, then he swung to the saddle, an easy grace in his movements she had not noticed before.

He turned when seated. "You ... do you come to us or go to him?"

"He is gone." Within her the words created a strange emptiness where none had been before. "He is gone."

"He will come back. Is he a fool to ride away from such a woman?"

She watched him ride away: his vest was patched, his boots were shabby and old, yet he was a man, this one. Her father would have been proud.

She stood very still in the empty yard, watching them out of sight. At last, as he crossed the ridge, Vicente lifted a hand. Then the shaggy pony went over the hill and out of sight.

Inside, the house looked empty and forlorn. She took the broom and began to sweep. Not to think ... that was the thing now. There was nothing to think about. There was only to wait.

What had she done? Ruined their lives for a strange gringo? A man who meant nothing to her and whom she had scarcely seen? She remembered the hard strength of his arms, his sudden strange gentleness ... she was a fool.

He was a drifting man, a man from the malpais, a gun fighter. And what had he told her? That she should join him or he would come back. But to join him would be to lead them to his hiding place and how could he come to her when it would mean his death? No matter. What she had done she had done. It was enough.

She was washing dishes left from breakfast when she heard them coming. She went to meet them, drying her hands on her apron.

There were nine of them, sour and dirty with sleeping in their clothes, wearied from long hours in the saddle. Mort Bayless was there ... she had heard stories about him ... Joe Sutton, Jack Sutton ... no friendly face among them.

Jack Sutton's face was ragged from lack of sleep. He looked drawn and mean. Beside him Ben Hindeman—as always—stolid, indomitable. A man who might have been cast from iron, before whom other men must bend or break.

"Where'd he go?" Hindeman asked the question, taking out the makings to build a cigarette.

"I don' know."

She made no attempt to evade the issue. If she could not defeat them she could at least face them with pride.

"He comin' back?"

She shrugged. "Back? ... Why he come back?"

Joe Sutton spoke into the momentary silence. "The sheep're gone, Ben. I think they've pulled out."

Ben Hindeman put the cigarette between his chapped lips. By God, this was a woman! The way she stood there ... no fear in her.

He considered it, taking his time. Ben Hindeman was a careful man and, outside his own family, a ruthless and cold-blooded man who lived for the brand. Old Bob Sutton had been the boss but now the mantle had fallen to Ben's shoulders as Old Bob had always expected.

Jack Sutton did not like that but there was little he could do. Among the sixty cowhands who rode for SB, not more than eight or nine would follow him, and none would risk a showdown with Hindeman. Direct, relentless and powerful, Hindeman wasted no effort. He destroyed what got in his way, smashing it down without malice or cruelty, simply because it was in the way.

There was something here that bothered Ben. There was in this Mexican girl something fierce, something tigerish and dangerous. She was not like his wife, who had the strength to yield and to endure, but this was a woman with an aggressive strength; she had a brain. That was something Jack would never understand.

It was because of this quality that Hindeman, who believed in no wasted effort, had left the Chaveros alone. They were better off in the canyons making their small living harmlessly from their sheep than hiding in the hills and living off SB stock.

What Jack did not realize was that this girl would fight and that not too many miles south there were Mexicans she could enlist to help her. And the best SB range lay on the south side of the border. It lay within the power of this girl to wreck the SB if she were hurt or angry and if she realized that she could. At the same time Hindeman knew the danger that could come from successful defiance of SB by Trace Jordan. Jordan must be found. He must be killed.

"Why did you stay?" he asked finally.

"Why should I go? This is my home." There was a fine insolence in her tone when she looked boldly at him and asked, "Do you fight women now?"

Mort Bayless' dry voice cut across the stillness. "Give me ten minutes with a quirt and spur. She'll talk."

Ben Hindeman looked at the tip of his cigarette, impatient with such talk. Mort was always bloody with women. Beat his own wife until she ran off and never came back. Mort had followed her ... maybe that was why she hadn't come back. But any fool should know this woman would not talk unless she chose.

"Ben?"

It was Jacob Lantz. The old tracker had squatted beside the house. "He'll come back, Ben."

Hindeman caught the look of something like fear that came to her face suddenly and was gone. Ben Hindeman was smart in his way. He was a one-woman man and that woman was his wife, on their ranch near Tokewanna, but he knew a woman when he saw one. *I'd come back*, he told himself, *by the Lord Harry, I'd come back.* "That's it," Ben said. "We'll wait."

Mort's face twisted with anger. *"Wait?"* He shoved his horse forward, almost knocking over Jacob Lantz. "I'll not wait! By the—!"

"Mort."

The chill voice arrested his movement, brought sanity to replace his sudden fury. Hindeman's shotgun was across his saddlebows and the twin muz-

71

zles had him in their eyes. "I'll give the orders here."

Mort hesitated, feeling something cold and ugly within him. Yet there was no room for argument with Ben Hindeman. The shotgun was no casual threat. "You wait, then," he said finally. "I'm going into town."

Maria Cristina walked into the house and sat down, her legs too weak to stand. Yet she had seen other things. There was a man with a bandaged face, like he had been shot through the cheeks. And Dave Godfrey was no longer with them. Trace Jordan was piling up a score.

Joe Sutton brought food into the house, piling it on the table. He faced her, hat in hand. "Will you cook? None of us are much at fixin' grub."

His manner was diffident, yet she was about to say no when she realized that well-fed men might relax and grow sleepy. "I'll cook," she said.

It was something to do and it would keep her from thinking. They believed Trace Jordan would come back—but would he? Because of her?

Six of them stayed, the others riding away after fresh horses. Hindeman, Jack and Joe Sutton, Lantz, Buck Bayless, and a dour-faced man she knew as Wes Parker stayed. Godfrey, she heard later, had been knocked over a cliff by falling rocks. He was dead.

She did not want Jordan to come back, yet she remembered the feel of his hands on her shoulders and the strange weakness that came over her when he touched her body. It was a feeling she had not known before and it frightened her.

She did not want to give so much to any man. To love was to give ... to put herself in the hands of a man and to one strange to her and to her ways. She would think no more of him. He was gone.

It had been enough and more than enough that other time. She had not been in love but was desperate for some wider life than that in their little corner of desert and mountains. With her father gone she was one more mouth to feed, so she had married Bud Hayes. She had never loved him but he had loved her and he had been a good man until he began to drink. But he was a weak man.

This man was different. There was something in him that made her believe even when she told herself she was a fool to listen. Men were liars. All of them.

She remembered how she had first seen him, lying across his half-opened blanket roll, his face ghastly, blood seeping from the broken wound in his side. He had seemed dead ... and then she saw him breathe.

He was gone now. He had gotten away. He would not come back. And if he did these men were waiting to kill him.

Buck Bayless pushed back from the table and looked at Maria Cristina with grudging admiration. "You can cook, Mex. I'll give you that."

She flashed him a sullen look and turned away. Behind her Joe Sutton got to his feet, saying a little self-consciously, "Thanks, Ma'am."

Wes Parker glanced at him scornfully but Hindeman added his thanks and Joe felt better. Only

73

Jack Sutton loitered at the table. The food *had* been good but Jack loitered because he could not convince himself that any mere Mexican girl could be cold to him. He stalled over his coffee, wanting to be alone with her.

Ben Hindeman came to the door after several minutes and said, with heavy sarcasm, "If you're going to stay in there, Jack, get away from the window. If Jordan sees you he'll never come in."

Irritably, Sutton moved.

Maria Cristina was thinking that tonight Jordan would not come back. Tonight he would wait for her. Tomorrow? He would wait tomorrow too. After that she must get away.

She came to herself with a start. She believed him! She was no foolish girl to listen to the talk of any cowpuncher. Yet it could not be that she was in love with this man. She could never truly love a gringo. Yet he had moved her as no man had and his hands upon her ... she hurriedly dismissed the thought and returned to cleaning up.

Behind her Jack Sutton sat with his hands shoved down behind his belt. He watched her move about the room, the flattening of her dress against her thighs, the way she moved her shoulders.

"You," he said, "comin' it high an' mighty, an' up there with him!"

She turned her back to the sideboard, her eyes taunting him. "You don't like that, do you? You think you big man! You think I should like you! Bah! You nothing! You animal! What woman want you? All you know is steal an' kill!"

He came off his chair with a lunge and slapped her across the mouth. The sound was like a pistol shot. Then he swung with the other palm and she grabbed behind her for a kitchen knife.

Before she could use it, Ben Hindeman sprang into the door. "Stop it!" he roared. "Damn you, Jack! Leave that girl alone!"

Sutton stopped, his face white with fury. He turned on Hindeman, his fingers spread, his face hungry with the lust to kill. "Don't talk to me like that, Ben! Some day I'll kill you!"

"All right." Ben Hindeman rolled his tobacco in his jaws. "You call it, Jack. Just any time." He jerked his thumb toward the door. "Right now you get out an' leave her alone. We ain't got time to let you mess things up by grabbing at her skirt. We're huntin' a man."

Jack Sutton waited while a man might have counted a slow twenty, then he walked by Hindeman and out the door. Something about Ben was too much for him. He had looked Jack right in the eye and never missed chewing his tobacco. He looked just the same when he watched a branding or bought a barrel of flour.

"Forget it, Ben. Only she gets under my skin."

Hindeman looked at the knife Maria Cristina gripped. "Yeah," he said dryly, "I can see where she might."

Hindeman left and Sutton turned in the door. "No matter what happens to Jordan, you're still here. After we're through with him nobody will care what happens to you. And when I get through with you there won't be anything for anybody."

Maria Cristina put down the knife. "I'll kill you," she said, utterly calm. "I'll kill you first."

The day drew on ... the waiting men watched the hills through the heat waves, watched a soaring buzzard. There was no other sound, no movement. Heat gathered in the canyon, sultry and thick. Jack Sutton swore bitterly and mopped his neck.

Buck Bayless sat in the shade near the lean-to barn and tossed pebbles at a panting lizard whose sides worked desperately at the hot, heavy air.

"It'll rain," Lantz said. "This'll bring rain."

They stayed in the shade and out of sight. There was no telling when Jordan might decide to return. Buck Bayless thought of what Lantz had said, that when Jordan came back they could have him. Bayless was remembering what had happened when they caught up with Jordan the first time.

There was something about Trace Jordan that was not good to contemplate. He was a tough savage fighting man who would fight like a cornered wolf.

Joe Sutton moved over beside him. "They had no business," he whispered to Bayless, "pullin' that stunt. Just like Jack an' Mort."

Buck Bayless had been thinking the same thing but he wasn't going to say it. Let Ben handle Jack. He wanted no part of him. But he was sure now that bunch of horses had been stolen, like Jordan claimed. "They sure tackled the wrong man," he said.

Bayless did not like this riding over the hot bitter hills, over these rocks shaped like flame. A cloud left a momentary shadow. It might rain, at that. It was overdue. "I'd like a beer," he said irritably. "I'm gettin' fed up."

Jack Sutton said nothing. He overheard the last remark and the sooner they all felt that way, the better. He wanted to be alone with that Mexican girl. He would show her then. He would show her plenty.

Lantz sat quietly in the deepest part of the shade. He always knew where shade would be deepest and last longest. He watched Jack Sutton from time to time, knowing what was in his mind.

Supper was a good meal again. Hindeman pushed back from the table but did not get up. Jack tried to wait him out, then gave up. Nobody could outwait Ben. He sat there stolid and immovable as a mountain. Exasperated, Jack gave up.

Ben rolled a smoke and lit up. He was no hand with women and never had been. He did not even understand his wife, with whom he had lived happily for some years. Yet some women would sell a man out. Some could be frightened. Some reached through their families. Yet how to reach this one?

He doubted it could be done but he was going to try. Ben Hindeman was a man of single purpose. He had one idea at a time and he never stopped until he had gone through, all the way. It was one of the things that held Jack Sutton from making a break. Ben wouldn't scare and he would be hard to kill.

"You love this man Jordan?" He asked it suddenly.

"Why you ask that?"

"Don't know, exactly. Curious, maybe. You done a lot for him."

"What I do? He is dying . . . I feex him up. I do it for you. I do it for anyone."

"You might, at that. You're a lot of woman." He turned it over in his mind, searching for something to take hold of. "Don't like us much, do you?"

"I should like you?" she shrugged, lifting her brows. "My father is keel by you. You try to drive us out. This is our country."

"We could change that," he began slowly. "Give you more land. The old man was dead set against sheep. I'm not." He looked up at her. "I could stake you. Go partners in a herd. You got enough family to handle 'em. We could split fifty-fifty."

He was sincere, she knew that. And if Hindeman was behind her, nobody else could object. Not out loud.

"What your wife say?" She was faintly amused.

Hindeman looked rueful. "Might cause trouble," he said, "the womenfolks don't like you much."

"For no reason. I don't bother them. I am good girl."

Ben Hindeman looked up. "I believe you," he said and was surprised not to have thought of it before. "Yes," he was thinking of all he had seen and heard, "I'm sure of it. But you know how women are. You look," he flushed a little, "you look sort of sexy."

"So? I am woman."

"Well, how's about the sheep? Is it a deal?"

"No."

"Because of my wife?" He hesitated. "I can handle that."

"Because of what you wish me to tell."

"Tell us where he is. I'll pull my men out of here and you can have the sheep."

"I do not know where he is."

"He say anything about comin' back?"

She hesitated and instantly knew her mistake. Quick knowledge came to Hindeman's eyes. "No," she said. "Why, come back?"

But she had hesitated too long. Hindeman got to his feet, feeling better. He would come back, all right. He would be worried about this girl. "You send for me when you want to talk. We'll get him, anyway. But you tell me where he is and I'll take care of the town. If I say you're all right, they'll treat you nice."

That was true. Hindeman's was the voice of authority. They might not like it but nobody would go against him. And Trace Jordan might try to come back and be killed. Yet she did not think of Hindeman's offer; she worried only that Jordan might come back and ride into a trap.

She made coffee and left it at the edge of the fire and then went to the door and told them of it. Then she went to her room but she did not undress. They would drink that coffee. They would drink it to keep themselves awake. But suppose they drank it and never wakened?

There were desert plants that held poison. Many of them she had known since she was a child. Rosa had told her of others. Rosa's mother had been a famous medicine woman among the Navajo.

But she was no murderess. But suppose they only slept? She did not immediately sleep but lay thinking. Somewhere out there in the desert stillness a pinnacle of rock pointed a beckoning finger at the sky . . . a quail called into the stillness . . . and there Trace Jordan waited for her.

Angrily she pushed her head into the pillow and after a while, she slept . . .

The problems Trace Jordan presented were the sort Jacob Lantz relished. Not since he had trailed renegade Apaches had he enjoyed his work so much. There were dozens of good hideaways in the Animas or Guadalupe Mountains but Jordan would push south into the wilderness of the San Luis. Jordan could live in that country because he could live like an Apache. But he would not go far until the girl was with him. So he told Hindeman.

"Nonetheless," Hindeman said, "we'll ride after those sheep and have a look. We'll take Joe with us."

Lantz looked thoughtfully at the house but said nothing. Leaving Jack behind was asking for trouble and Lantz wanted nothing to happen to that girl. She was his best chance to catch Jordan. An hour after daybreak the three rode away. Jack Sutton rolled a cigarette and watched them go.

Wes Parker sat down, looking expectant. Buck Bayless rubbed his jaw nervously. Maria Cristina saw them and she had seen Hindeman go. She took the butcher knife and placed it under a cloth on the sideboard.

Boots grated on gravel and Jack Sutton stepped in. He was smiling a thin smile but there was no smile in his eyes. "Ben's gone," he said.

"*Si.*" Maria Cristina's eyes were watchful. "I know."

"I been waitin' for a chance like this."

"You are coward. You afraid of him."

Sutton stepped into the room. "No, not afraid of him. Just smart. Ben gets the work done. He keeps trouble off my shoulders, so I let him have his way."

"You get out. You no business here."

Jack Sutton smiled. It was not a nice smile. "I've plenty of business here. I'm going to teach you a lesson."

He walked around the table and stopped in front of her. She made no move to escape. Her eyes watchful, she merely waited, showing no expression.

He lifted his hand, palm open, and then he struck her. Maria Cristina's eyes widened but she merely stared at him, the print of the blow on her cheek. Her very impassiveness infuriated him. He doubled his fist and, as he did, she jerked the knife from under the cloth. He caught the gleam and whipped back just as the point of the knife ripped up through his shirt.

Stepping back, he tripped over a chair and fell. Instantly Maria Cristina was around him and out of the door. He leaped up and grabbed at her but tripped over the chair again. Then she was through the door and running for the gully.

Wes Parker sprang to catch her but she turned on him and slashed with the knife. He sprang back, swearing, blood streaming from his arm.

The delay had given Sutton time to get to her.

Evading the knife, he knocked her down. Before she could rise he kicked the blade from her hand.

She got up, moving back, her eyes alive with hatred, but he moved in on her and, disdaining her blows, picked her up and carried her back to the house and dumped her. Instantly, she sprang back and stood panting, watching him like an animal at bay.

Outside Wes was swearing, blood streaming from his arm. Buck Bayless stared at the house, his face sweating. He ran his tongue over his lips.

"Don't stand there like a fool!" Parker yelled. "Fix up my arm!"

Bayless started toward Parker but his attention was on the house. Inside, Maria Cristina stood against the sideboard watching Sutton come toward her.

"I've been waiting for this chance," Sutton said. "And I'll use it." He struck her and then, methodically, he began to beat her. Blood trickling from a cut lip, she tried to escape him but he came after her, his fury mounting with each blow.

"I'll kill you!" he said hoarsely. "You—"

"Jack!" That was Buck's voice. Sutton stopped, fist lifted. Outside he heard the rattle of horses' hoofs. Angrily he struck out but Maria Cristina was watching and she sprang back, falling to the floor.

As Lantz watched, Ben Hindeman was getting from the saddle. Sutton strode from the house. Hindeman and Sutton faced each other and for a long tense minute, neither spoke. Then Hindeman went past and into the house.

Maria Cristina was just rising from the floor but

she lacked the strength and fell back. Hindeman swore softly as he saw her bruised and bloody face. He took her arm to help her up but she jerked free and rose by herself. "You are animal! All are animal! Cowards! You fight women!"

Hindeman's face showing his shame, he turned quickly and went outside. Jack Sutton was loitering, waiting for him. Hindeman saw the readiness in Sutton. He was ready for a showdown and the very idea made Hindeman impatient. This was no time for that kind of trouble. "Are you crazy?" he demanded. "We need that girl. You kill her and where are we?"

Sutton turned on Lantz when Hindeman had passed. "It was you brought him back, damn you! One of these days I'll—"

Lantz was chewing a blade of grass. His little eyes were utterly cold. "When you try, you better make sure. I ain't so fancy with a hand-gun but I'll kill you, Jack! I'll hunt you like I'd hunt a varmint an' I'll kill you!"

Jack Sutton strode past him to his horse. The fools! The damned fools! He got into the saddle and rode out of the canyon at breakneck speed.

Hindeman returned. "If he bothers you, Jake, you come to me."

The old man turned black eyes to Hindeman. He spat. "You better take care o' *him*, Ben. Not me."

Hindeman stared at his big hands. What was this chase doing to them? Tearing the outfit apart, that was what it was doing. And it had been Jack and Mort and their crowd who brought it all on them, stealing those horses. It was just that some men had the killer streak in them that nothing but death could stop.

Those mountains down there, the Sierra de San Luis. That could well be where Jordan was. If he got away across the malpais into the Sierra Madre they must just as well forget him. But they did not dare. Nobody realized more than he how many were the enemies around them. Old Bob had ridden roughshod over people and his nephews had been worse. Moreover, there were people who wanted their range. The slightest evidence of weakness and the SB would be only a memory.

Turning on his heels, he walked back to the house. Maria Cristina's face was swollen from the heavy blows. It was only barely recognizable. "Will you still cook?" he asked.

She stared into his blocky granite-hard face. "I cook," she said and turned from him.

Later he saw her walk from the house with her basket and go to the patch of squaw cabbage. He watched her, then let her go. She was in plain sight there and couldn't get away.

She stooped to pick some bread-root, taking the starchy taproot from the ground. She moved on, then, and stopped for a moment near a dark-leaved plant with white flowers. And then she walked on. Returning to the house, she set about preparing a meal. Several times men came to the door for coffee but she turned them away, saying it was not ready.

Wes Parker had been sent to town. Jack Sutton had not returned. Only Lantz, Buck Bayless and Hindeman were there.

Finally she dished up the food and they ate. She watched them for a while, then poured more coffee. After that she hastily packed sandwiches and other food in an old flour sack and nobody watched her. She was always moving about, always busy.

Frightened now, she listened anxiously for Sutton's return. Several times she glanced out, seeing cigarettes glowing in the dark. She heard a queer laugh, then a chuckle. Bayless called out to Hindeman but there was no reply. She waited until no cigarettes glowed near the barn, nor was there any sound of voices.

Crossing to the barn, she found them sprawled on the ground, sleeping. She took a Winchester from one of the men, took cartridge belts from two and a box of .44 shells from inside the barn door. At the corner of the barn she untied a horse and, making every move count, led him to the house and loaded food and blankets. Getting into the saddle, she walked the horse away from the house and, when well away, broke into a trot.

All was still . . . and then Jack Sutton rode out of the darkness. He glanced at the snoring men and then with a chuckle he turned to Maria Cristina's trail and started off at a walk. Behind him there was silence. The lights from the house shone on the men who slept heavily in their drugged sleep.

Jack Sutton was only to a degree a family man. Many a man who dared not face him with a gun might have shot him down from ambush had he not been backed by the Sutton-Bayless outfit. The family was a protective cloak.

Ben Hindeman, on the other hand, had a fierce loyalty to Old Bob, whose daughter he married, and to the brand. He was wise enough to know that at the first sign of weakness the wolves would close in for the kill.

Jack Sutton was not thinking of this. He had lately undergone that final and subtle change that came to many gunmen. At first, such a man may suffer when he kills but the second comes easier and by degrees the gunman becomes contemptuous of his victims and kills casually or for the love of it. Yet his own danger increases, for now men wish to kill him. So he becomes a destroyer with a hand ever ready to grasp the gun.

In Maria Cristina he had found someone he could not frighten, nor could he believe she was innocent of blame during those visits on the shelf. What he wished now was to find Jordan and kill him before her eyes. He wanted to break her spirit and, at the same time, to prove his own superiority. So he was in no hurry to catch up, wanting her only to lead him to Jordan.

It was very hot when the sun came up and the country through which Maria Cristina rode became increasingly dry. Yet by an hour after dawn she was sure she was being followed.

This was dry country and behind her she had seen a plume of dust. It was such a dust cloud as would be left by one rider. And that could only mean that Jack Sutton was behind her.

Twice she varied her direction, choosing a likely route, then an unlikely one. She used every subterfuge she could think of and she deliberately avoided water holes. All that morning she refused herself even a swallow of water, although twice she paused to sponge the mouth of her horse.

She told herself she was going to Trace Jordan for two reasons: because sooner or later she believed she would be killed by Jack Sutton and because she was afraid Jordan would return.

Dust mounted in her nostrils. Dust caked her face and sifted over her clothing. Sweat streaked the dust. The horse plodded wearily on.

Maria Cristina did not believe she could deceive Jacob Lantz for long but she might lose Jack Sutton. His very confidence might defeat him. Yet she must try to outwit Lantz as well and when they reached a long rocky shelf, she decided the time had come. She pulled up and dismounted.

Jacob Lantz was the first to awaken. The sky was gray when he opened his eyes and then, as realization dawned, he sprang up. Swearing bitterly, he ran to the house. The light still burned but a quick search revealed everything.

"Gone!" he shouted. "She got away! Tricked like a lot of tenderfeet!"

Ben Hindeman's head ached violently but he hurriedly saddled up. There were extra horses in the barn and at the last minute, Joe Sutton returned to join them.

Lantz went to his cup and found the dregs of what he had drunk. He touched his tongue to it, tasting. *"Toloache!"* he spat viciously and went swiftly to his horse.

"Somethin' here," he said a few minutes later. "Jack's followin' her."

Shrewd in the ways of hunted and hunting men, Lantz understood why Jack Sutton hung back. He believed she would lead him to Jordan. Would she do it?

Through the hot still morning he worked out their trails, yet he noticed Jack's only in passing. It was the girl he must follow.

When her trail finally petered out on the rocky shelf, Jack was already gone. Somewhere back along the route she had tricked him. Lantz worked patiently. He found the tiny white scar made by a hoof on sandstone but it was the last one.

He circled, then circled wider still. Neither heat nor thirst disturbed him. The glare of the sun squinted his eyes but he continued to search. He stopped suddenly ... a tiny red thread. He chuckled as he picked it up.

"What's so funny?" Bayless demanded irritably.

"Gal's smart. Tied rags around her horse's hoofs."

No use to try and follow her now. There would be few marks, maybe miles apart. Working out such a trail might take weeks. But it would not be necessary.

Cottonwood Creek was dry at this time of year. So was Cowboy Spring. Somebody had blown out the dam at millsite, so where, then, would she go?

Jordan had been with her before he left. She knew she would be followed so she would try to lead them off the trail. So then, he could figure that the trail was faked. To circle around to a water hole in any other direction would not take a day or two days but a week. Therefore, somewhere in that vast expanse to the south, Trace Jordan had to be waiting for her.

One by one he ticked off the possibilities, then ... "Got an idea," he said. They mounted and followed him. Yet three hours later when they rode up to Wolf Pen Tank there were no tracks around and green scum covered the water. Not even a stray steer ...

Angrily Lantz bit off a chew of tobacco. Now where in tarnation!

He swore bitterly, remembering. Old Chavero had once holed up for several days at that intermittent stream that came out of the ground near the pinnacles. "That's it!" he said. "That's it!"

Bayless swore. "How long's this goin' on?"

"Come on," Hindeman said, "we'll find 'em."

They left Wolf Pen at a brisk trot. The afternoon was well along and in a short time it would be cool and they could move faster.

At dusk Trace Jordan pulled the picket pin and saddled up. Then he led the red horse to the path that led out the back way. He was restless and worried, unable to sit down or relax. His wound was itching ... it must be healing. He drank more water and moved to where he could look down the trail. There was nothing in sight.

Yet he had almost dozed off when he heard the sound of a walking horse.

He came to his feet, Winchester in hand. Twice as he listened the horse stumbled. It was very tired. He shifted the rifle to his left hand and touched his pistol. He moved to the patch of mead-ow, passing soundlessly through the grass. The moon was just coming over the rocks and the meadow was bathed in pale light. Ghostlike the horse and rider materialized from the dakness.

Jordan started to her, seeing her hair against the light. Then faintly, far or close he could not guess, he heard another sound.

"You are here?" She spoke softly, yet her words carried. He did not reply. Somebody or something was out there in the darkness. Somebody who also listened.

She walked her horse deeper into the clearing. She made a silent lonely figure, like an Indian woman on her horse. "You are here?" There was a plaintive lost tone in her voice that twisted his heart.

He waited and in the stillness there was no sound. She sat still upon her horse, waiting for some response. He could almost feel the hope going out of her. Was he, as she must have be-lieved, only another man who would ride away? Had he taken her help, let her get into a corner and then left her alone? Desperately he wanted to speak, to cry out, to—

"No," it was another voice, "he ain't here. But I am."

A tall man in a conical hat stepped from the shadows. She tried to start her horse as he grabbed at it but the horse was too tired to move quickly. Sutton grabbed the bridle and jerked the horse around and then he reached for Maria.

Trace Jordan picked up a small stick and tossed

FLINT

IF HE HAD TO DIE, AT LEAST IT WOULD BE ON HIS TERMS...

Get a taste of the true West, beginning with the tale of *FLINT* FREE for 15 Days

Hunted by a relentless hired gun in the lava fields of New Mexico, Flint *"settled down to a duel of wits that might last for weeks...Surprisingly, he found himself filled with zest for the coming trial...So began the strange duel that was to end in the death of one man, perhaps two."*

If gripping frontier adventures capture your imagination, welcome to The Louis L'Amour Collection! It's a handsome, hardcover series of thrilling sagas by the world's foremost Western authority and author.

Each novel in The Collection is a true-to-life portrait of the Old West, depicted with gritty realism and striking detail. Each is enduringly bound in rich, Sierra-brown leatherette, with padded covers and gold-embossed titles. And each may be examined and enjoyed for 15 days. FREE. You are never under any obligation; so mail the card at right today.

Now in handsome Heritage Editions

Each matching 6" x 9" volume in The Collection is bound in rich Sierra-brown leatherette, with padded covers and embossed gold title... creating an enduring family library of distinction.

it into the brush a dozen feet away. It lit in the brush and instantly the man by the horse turned and Jordan saw moonlight on a gun barrel.

Sutton waited, his gun poised. Then he relaxed slowly. "Animal," he said aloud. He turned toward Maria Cristina. "Now I'm goin' to finish what I started."

She was still too close to him. There was too much risk of her being hit if shooting started. Jordan picked up a small stone and tossed it into the brush across the clearing. Sutton froze in place, listening. Then he holstered his gun. "Get down," he said, "or I'll pull you down."

Maria Cristina had sat still, apparently too weary to move, too defeated to try. Now she moved suddenly. She threw her leg over the horse and dropped to the ground on the opposite side. She slapped the horse and he lunged. Sutton sprang back and Maria Cristina dropped into the blackness at the edge of the brush and was absolutely still.

Jack Sutton stood alone in the clearing, staring at the shadows, listening for her breathing. "Do you no good," he said conversationally. "I'll have it my way now. Ben ain't here to stop me."

There was a faint whisper of grass around Trace Jordan's feet as he moved. Trace Jordan was going to kill a man. He had to kill and not be killed for she must not be left alone with Jack Sutton. He stopped and he knew Sutton could see him.

"Who is it?" Sutton demanded. "Buck? Ben?"

Tension was building but more for Sutton than

for him. He knew whom he faced; Sutton saw only a shadow in the night.

"Speak up!" Sutton said impatiently. "Who are you?"

"I reckon I'm the man you been hunting," Jordan said, "unless you hunt only women."

CHAPTER FOUR

The night was cool. Jack Sutton stood very still, hearing the slow heavy beat of his heart. He wished he could see Trace Jordan. This shadowy figure worried him. There was no personality there, only something dark, indefinite, indistinct.

Never, since the beginning, had he seen this man. His partner he had killed and he had helped to pursue him and bring him to this moment but never once in all that time had he actually seen Trace Jordan.

You could not look into his eyes; you could not measure the man. It disturbed Sutton but did not make him less confident.

"I figure you're one of those who murdered my partner," Jordan said.

Sutton wondered if Jordan could see his gun hand. It was dangling at his side but he began to inch it higher. "Sure!" His voice was taunting. "I'm one of them. Fact is, it was my idea."

His hand was at the bottom of the holster as he

spoke. He had only to bend his elbow to grasp the butt. He bent his elbow suddenly. His hand grasped his gun butt and suddenly he was choking with the lust to kill. He drew—

The bullets smashed him in the belly like two fists, a hard one-two that set him back on his heels. He put his left foot back to steady himself and started to lift his gun but when he got his hand up he found it was empty.

Confused, he stared blindly at his hand and then his knees buckled and he fell. His body from the waist down was numb, yet his brain was alive and clear. He tried to speak, to see the face of the man who stood there, watching him. He tried to frame words but then the notion faded . . . this then was how it felt to die.

The last thing he remembered was the wet grass on his face.

Trace Jordan walked forward, circling a little, knowing his bullets had gone true, yet wary as always, taking no chances, estimating the danger of the man who lay there.

"Maria Cristina?" Then she was coming toward him. "We must ride now. They'll be coming." He gestured. "Take his horse. He hasn't covered the ground yours has."

Into the desert they rode. Sand and more sand. Rock, Spanish dagger, yucca, ocotillo and broken lava. It was a brutal heat-baked corner of hell.

The cacti cast weird shadows in the moonlit night and a low wind moaned in the scattered clumps of brush. They rode in silence, knowing there was no returning now. Another Sutton had died and made another mark against them.

The Sierra de San Luis pointed a rocky finger into the wastelands south of the border. It was Apache country and it was the desert and the desert can kill. This was the land that time and again had defeated armies of the United States. This was the land of the peccary and coyote, the land of the rattler and the scorpion, of the prickly pear and the cholla.

In the moonlight even more than by day the desert is a place of weird and strange beauty. One can live in the desert. There are plants that provide food; there are plants and places that provide water. But if one does not conform to the desert's pattern, one can die in the desert.

They did not talk. When the first light of dawn came he saw how her face was bruised and swollen and for the first time Trace Jordan was glad that he had killed a man. Yet she did not complain, she sat her horse well and rode straight on into the awful wilderness to the south. He looked back but saw nothing. No riders, no dust, no movement.

Sweat trickled down his face and down his body under his shirt. Twice within three hours great canyons split the desert floor. They descended into them and they emerged from them. And when he looked back a second time there was a dust cloud. There were two dust clouds.

This was wilderness, raw, untamed. There were no villages and no ranches. It was the land of the Apache, the most dreaded guerilla fighter the world has yet known. When it was almost noon he drew up and they dismounted, sponging out the mouths and nostrils of their horses. And then they walked.

Dust settled on their faces and necks. Jordan felt his neck growing raw from the chafing of his collar, stiffened as it was by sweat and dust. His head ached, his mouth was dry, yet they pushed on and the heat waves moved in closer around them, blotting out the distance, leaving only a vast shimmering waste.

Twice, for short times, they rested. Each time the dust clouds seemed closer.

"You know this country?" he asked.

"Down here? No."

"There is a place, the Canyon de Los Embudos," he said. "Do you know it?"

"It is an Apache place."

"There is water," he said, "and a place to hide."

The country became increasingly broken and again they mounted. Yet before many miles had passed Sutton's horse began to stumble. The big red horse Jordan rode had rested well and fed well. The distance seemed as nothing to him. They dismounted again and walked on but Sutton's horse fell and lay there in the sun.

"Take the food and the rifle," Jordan said. "We'll leave him."

"He will die?"

"No ... after the sun goes down he'll get up. He will find water then or join them when they come up."

So they walked on but his strength had not returned and after a while the horizon began to weave and dance before him and the mountains became like liquid and he went to his knees. He got up at once and started on, tearing his collar wider. The gun belts and pistols chafed his thighs.

They looked back and there were no dust clouds. He looked ahead and three Apaches on ragged ponies stared stone-faced into their eyes. It was too late for the rifle and he did not know if his hand was strong enough to hold a gun.

From under his black hat brim he looked at them. Three tough men of the desert, their finely muscled bodies shaped like the land itself, of rock and sinew. Being Apaches, they would have seen the dust clouds and they would be wondering about them.

Jordan gestured at their back trail. "Enemy," he said, then indicated Maria Cristina's battered face and touched his gun.

They were impassive, their black eyes studying him. He was sunburned and as dark as any of them, only his eyes were gray. Maria Cristina looked at them but said nothing. Her man was talking and this was man's business.

"*Indio?*" An Apache pointed at her.

Jordan gave the sign for half, then indicated himself with the same sign. This last was not true but he had the features and could have been and the idea might help.

The Apache with the red headband turned and pointed. "*Embudos,*" he said.

"*Si,*" Jordan replied and when the Apaches drew aside, they went on, walking slowly. Neither of them spoke, neither made a sound until they were hidden in an arroyo. Then he swung quickly to the saddle and with Maria Cristina behind him rode rapidly until several miles were behind them.

Hours later, his feet aching and his body utterly exhausted, he was still moving. Yet now the terrain had changed. They had entered a weird jungle of Spanish dagger, cholla and Joshua, all broken by the remains of an ancient lava flow. The spaces between the cacti and the fallen black chunks of lava were crowded with brittle bush.

For what must have been six or seven miles they inched their way through this barrier, at times at a loss as to how to go forward; then, mounting a hill amid a thick forest of cholla, they suddenly looked into a ravine that was startlingly and incredibly lovely.

Below them was water. Not a little water but a large clear pool surrounded by jutting lava. Shading the pool were sycamore, ash, willow and buckthorn. And down near the edge of the pool were several small open places where they could see the remains of old fires.

Dismounting, Jordan led the way down the steep path to the water's edge. Following along the shore under an overhang of lava they came to a small clearing among the trees, completely shaded and masked from view by a curtain of willows. Here they stopped. With almost the last of his strength Jordan stripped the saddle from the red horse and put him on a picket rope.

Then without a word he stretched out and went immediately to sleep, a sleep through which horses raced and guns barked and where he was endlessly falling over blocks of lava into acres of cholla.

When he awakened it was dark and cold but a blanket had been thrown over him. Faintly he smelled a wood fire. He rolled over and sat up.

"There is food," Maria Cristina spoke from the shadows. "By the fire."

He stumbled to the edge of the pool and bathed himself, mopping his face and body dry with his shirt. Wrapping himself in a blanket, he went to the fire.

There was a pot of stew and he ate hungrily, then ate from a stick of tortillas. Then he sat down, looking at the moonlight's reflection on the dark water, listening to the night sounds and drinking coffee.

"S'pose Lantz knows this place?" he asked.

"Who knows?"

She was silent for a time. "He is a devil ... but not so bad as the rest."

They needed rest, the horse needed rest. To go on in the night was out of the question. They would just take a chance. They must stay.

"My father ... he knew of this place. It is a place of the *Indios*, of the Apaches. They come here to make talk—but not often, I think."

He got up stiffly, every muscle complaining, and going to his saddle he got his bed roll. He spread out his blankets and took off his boots.

When he had stretched out he said, "I am sorry about your face."

"It is nothing."

"The man I killed?"

"Si . . . Jack Sutton."

He drew the blanket about his shoulders and settled down to rest. Once, lifting his head, he glanced around. She sat unmoved and unmoving, her profile etched sharply against the sky beyond the lake. He started to speak, then changed his mind and lay down. In a moment he was breathing deeply and steadily.

Maria Cristina hunched the blanket around her shoulders and looked at the water. She said nothing; she thought nothing; she was at this moment an Indian, at one with her world.

Fifteen miles back, huddled under an escarpment of sandstone, Hindeman and his men made dry camp. It had been a day of defeat, of heat, dust and cacti.

At dawn they had found Jack Sutton. He had been shot dead and it had been good shooting. His gun, unfired, lay near his hand. Looking down at the body, Buck Bayless felt a moment of shock, of near terror. What kind of a man was Jordan?

Wounded unto death, he escaped. Days later he came from hiding and left not a ghost of a trail and now he had slain Jack Sutton. Buck Bayless felt his courage draining from him. He felt sick and whipped.

Wes Parker touched his tongue to his lips and stole a careful look at Hindeman. Yet he knew Hindeman would go on. It was a trait of Hindeman's that he had admired. Now he cursed it.

Ben Hindeman could feel no remorse. Sooner or later he would have had to kill Jack Sutton himself or be killed. Now the man was dead, finished. "Woman crazy," he said aloud. "If he left her alone, he'd be alive."

"She's a curse," Buck Bayless said resentfully. "She'll be the death of us all. Let her go, I say, and good riddance."

Ben Hindeman was angrily impatient. "We can let her go," he said, "but we can't let him go. If one man can wipe his feet on the Sutton-Bayless outfit, we won't last out the year. We kill him or we all go."

He swung a wide arm at the country. "There's fifty outfits in Arizona and New Mexico who want our graze. There's two or three mighty near strong enough to do it. Like John Slaughter . . . that's why I kept Jack an' Mort from going that way."

They were still there when Mort Bayless came in with four men. These were the tough ones, the men with a reason to want Trace Jordan dead. Mort Bayless had used an argument they could understand. "We got him runnin'," he said. "You think he'll let up if we quit? Not by a damn sight!

"He'll bide his time an' he'll come back. Folks will talk; he'll know who got his horses. He'll hunt down every man-jack of us, you'll see!"

He knew their fears because he knew his own. This was a danger they understood. Jordan was a tough man and they had been fools to listen to Jack Sutton. Beside the fire they hunkered down and made war talk.

"Where'll they go?" Hindeman asked Lantz.

The old man spat into the fire. "No tellin'. With the Mex gal we could figure some but Jordan's takin' the lead now an' he knows where he's goin'. This here desert is out of my knowin'. Might be a sight of places around if a body knew 'em."

He took a pull at the coffee. "You been thinkin', Ben? This here's 'Pache country. We get caught down here an' we're in genuine trouble."

"No matter. We'll find him."

"Worse'n huntin' a needle in a haystack," Buck Bayless complained. "We'd have to hunt up ever' canyon. Take us ten year."

"Hadn't better," Ben Hindeman replied dryly. "Your wife will forget you in that time."

Wes Parker lifted himself to an elbow. "I'm goin' back. I'm catchin' me that Mex kid. If that gal knows a hideout down here, that kid should know."

Ben Hindeman considered that. He did not like to have anyone abused but the situation was getting out of hand. They were losing time and the ranch needed them. All had work that needed doing. Moreover, for the first time he was finding an element of doubt. The increased caution of Lantz was part of it.

"All right, Wes. Take Buck with you. Maybe he'll be better huntin' a kid than a man."

"Aw, Ben!" Buck protested plaintively. "That ain't no—"

"Shut up!" Ben was exasperated. "Jake, you do something about where they might go. Meanwhile we'll get some sleep."

Lantz spat out his chewing. "Better set guards," he said, "them broncho Apaches might want to collect some horses."

Buck Bayless retired to his blankets vastly satisfied. What he wanted was less alkali and more beer. To hell with Jordan!

Before daybreak Trace Jordan crawled from his blankets into the pre-dawn chill. He slung his gun belts across his hips, then pulled on his boots. The fire had died to thin gray ashes, so he gathered a few dried leaves from under the trees and some dried-out branches of the curl-leaf, which makes no smoke.

Maria Cristina lay huddled in her blankets where he had last seen her, so he broke sticks quietly and fed them into the flames. He dipped water from the lake and placed the coffee pot on a stone by the fire to grow hot.

This place was well hidden. It was surrounded by a jungle of cholla, sometimes called jumping cactus, one of the most vicious of all the desert's plants. There were cat-claw, organ pipe and a few barrel cacti.

Finding a way through the maze would not be easy. He had stumbled upon it himself and even that trail had been difficult to follow.

When breakfast was ready he went to her and bent over to awaken her, yet even as he stooped, her eyes opened suddenly, dark and beautiful, ringed with black lashes. Her expression was, at that moment, unreadable. He started to reach for her, then drew back. "Got some coffee ready," he said.

Their eyes held for a long moment and then she said, "All right. I come."

Birds whistled and talked in the brush and the morning air was fresh and cool. He could smell the faint scent of ironwood in bloom but doubted his senses, for the season was late. Yet many desert plants bloomed according to rainfall and with small regard for seasons.

Maria Cristina came to the fire and accepted coffee from him. Her face was somber, and she stood, feet apart, holding the cup in both hands. "It is quiet," she said suddenly.

"Yes ... I like it here."

She drank her coffee, then ate. He gathered more firewood and then walked back up the trail to study the approaches by daylight. Only two or three places offered access to the water and all were in full view of their camp site.

From the top of the knoll he studied the surroundings. There was a nearby mesa that offered danger but few approaches through the cactus barrier. At the top of the knoll in a place he could work without being seen he assembled a few rocks into a low barrier.

There was grass for the horse and they had food for several days. They could wait.

Maria Cristina had washed their few dishes and had hot water on when he returned. She was putting creosote leaves into the water and when they had steeped for some time she bathed her bruised face in the water.

All day long they rested, sleeping much of the time. Occasionally, from the top of the knoll, Jordan made a reconnaissance of the country around, always keeping himself under cover. He could see but a short distance and in that distance there was nothing alive but the birds, who seemed very busy among the cacti. Without doubt the Sutton-Bayless riders were somewhere around. By this time they should be closing in. The thought increased his restlessness but there would be nowhere that would offer them more than they had at present.

Maria Cristina bathed her bruised face several times and in the late afternoon went into the thicket to find herbs that could be eaten to fill out their slender supply of food.

At dusk Trace Jordan took his Winchester and worked his way to the top of the mesa where he sat for a long time, studying the country. From there he could see for miles in all directions, yet it was not until he started to get up to return that he caught sight of the distant spot of red.

Far beyond the limits of the cholla forest, it was without doubt a campfire. And it would be ten or twelve miles away. Catching the last of the fading light, he worked his way back down the mesa to the oasis.

"They're out there," he said.

"We stay?"

"If we don't move we won't make tracks."

They did not have to worry about their own fire. He knew the distance a blaze can be seen at night but their own camp was so deep in the canyon and so well surrounded by trees and brush that it could not be seen fifty yards off. Their best chance was to sit tight.

She sat close by the fire, its light touching her somber face. Some of the swelling had gone and the bruises were changing color. Yet now she looked remote, lonely.

"What will you do?" he asked suddenly. "You cannot go back."

She shrugged.

"Stay with me."

She looked up, her eyes flashing, almost angry. "With you? For why? Why I go with you?"

"You're my woman, Maria Cristina."

"I am nobody's woman."

"You're my woman. Get used to the idea."

She glared at him, then said contemptuously, "For why am I your woman? Because I help you? I do it for a dog. All right ... I am in trouble. They hate me. I hate them too.

"I'm not going to let you go, Maria."

"You have nothing to say if I go or stay."

He got his bed roll and opened it out near the fire. He stretched out, leaning on one elbow. He fed small sticks into the fire and tried to find words to say what was in his mind.

She could never go back now and because of him. Because of him she was lost to her family and yet he knew it was no sense of obligation that made him feel as he did.

It had been a long time since he had talked to women and words did not come easily to him and yet he knew, desperately, that he must find words to reach this woman. He must make her realize that he loved her, that he really wanted her. He thought of many things to say but they found no shape on his lips. They all seemed empty and meaningless.

He was learning that to speak of love is not easy when the feeling is deep and strong.

She lifted her eyes suddenly and looked across the small fire at him. "You think because I come here with you that I am your woman? Well ... I am not."

"I need you, Maria."

"You need *me?* You need a woman ... any woman. Then you ride on. Maybe sometime again you need a woman, you find one again." She looked at him with a taunt in her eyes. "Anyway, I don't think you need a woman very often."

He ignored the comment and relaxed. "Trouble is," he mused, "I let you ride that horse. I should have made you walk ... all the way."

He sat up and began to roll a smoke. "And I should have made you carry the pack too."

She glared at him. He took a stick from the fire and lighted his cigarette. "A good woman needs to work," he said. "They're unhappy if they aren't working. Keep 'em busy, that's what I say."

"You!" she said witheringly. "What do you know?"

He drew deep on the cigarette. "I know you're my woman, Maria Cristina. Maybe I'll make you my woman tonight."

"Maybe you die." She looked at him, her eyes fierce and proud.

"Sure," he said, "my mistake was letting you ride. If you had followed behind with a pack on your back you'd be happy now. Next time we move, you walk."

"You think you strong!"

The moon had risen beyond the mesa and the cholla needles were like white flowers in the strange light, a beautiful white like a garden of flowers ... a garden of death. A bat dipped and darted through the air and out across the pool something splashed in the water.

He rolled up on his elbow again. "Always figured to get myself a ranch. Just a few cows and some horses. Mostly horses. Nothing real big, just a place that's mine. I want my own home.

"I always wanted a place with a view. One where I can see all the way into tomorrow ... a place with a long trail leading to it with my house at the end of the road. I want to see my own horses feeding in my own meadow. I want to see some youngsters growing up."

He smoked the cigarette down to a butt, then nursed the last few drags before tossing it into the flames. "Been a long time since I had a home. Take me awhile to get halter-broke again ... but I could do it."

A coyote spoke the moon, his shrill cries mounting in crescendo, then dying away in echoes against the mesa wall.

"A man can't make it alone. Needs him a woman. These here city women, they look mighty nice but a man out here needs a woman who can walk beside him, not behind him."

Maria Cristina said nothing. Her eyes were a little softer, perhaps, her hands relaxed. Some of the tenseness seemed to have gone out of her.

"You an' me, we could make it. I'm a hand with horses and I know where there's some pretty good wild stock. Buy us a stallion maybe, good blood. Might get a Morgan.

"Man can do a lot worse than raise horses. This is horse country, an' down here they'll always have a need for horse stock. With a Morgan stallion a man could breed some fair stuff in a few years. First year or two might not be easy. Reckon I couldn't offer you much ... not right off. Nothin' much but work and a home."

"I have always work."

She did not look at him but she spoke. He glanced across the fire at her but she did not meet his eyes and then suddenly she got up and started away.

"A man should stick to what he knows," he said, to her departing back. "I know horses ... maybe not so much about women."

He made no move to follow her. She seemed to wish to be alone, to think, perhaps. Well, it was true of himself. He took his rifle and walked off toward the path, not knowing if she saw him or not.

The forest of cholla lay like a fluffy white cloud when he climbed the mesa, yet a cloud composed of thorns, invisible in the moonlight, but ready to rend and tear. The Indians and the Mexicans thought the bunches of needles would lean toward a hand that came close, would jump at bare flesh. He doubted it but there were times when it seemed to happen.

Atop the mesa he looked off into the vast mysterious distances of the desert.

He thought of the silent girl beside the pool. He

had known few women and certainly none at all like Maria Cristina. Yet it seemed to him she was like some horses he had handled, shying from a hand that would caress, hungry to be petted, yet afraid to be trapped, to be caught, to be cheated.

He stared out across the desert. Wherever the fire was, it was gone now ... no ... it was there, winking from time to time across the distance.

Around that fire were belted men, tough men, dedicated to hunting him down. Between those men and himself there could be no peace. It was a bloody and desperate fight for survival, a fight that had driven him until soon he would have his back to the wall, where he must stand and fight.

It was a pity that Maria Cristina was involved, yet had she not chosen to involve herself he would be dead. He would have died on that mesa shelf, alone.

All the more reason he should protect her now, yet it would be useless to tell her to take the horse and go. She would merely look at him with that haughty contempt and remain right where she was.

So what to do? If they escaped from here, where could they go? Deeper into Mexico? He did not know the trails, although he knew this area of Sonora and much of Chihuahua. And he was sure she did not know the way. Every foot of travel to the south would be dangerous because of marauding Apaches.

To go back across the border at some point distant from the Sutton-Bayless stronghold?

Yet with one horse it would be a dangerous trip.

Only luck and the strength of the red horse had brought them this far and neither could last.

After long thought he got up and went back down the trail to the water. Only the fire glowed ... there was no sound and no movement. His bed lay beside the fire where he had unrolled it but of Maria Cristina there was no sign.

He spoke her name into the silence ... nothing. He said her name again, louder this time and with rising fear.

No sound, nothing ...

He ran swiftly to her bed. It was there but she was not. He called her name loudly and only the echo replied. He ran to the water's edge. Something caught his eye ... a fragment of cloth on a branch of ironwood.

A good-sized fragment, as though she had deliberately hooked it over the branch to leave a clue.

There were two paths that way. He ran along the nearest, praying his choice was right. He ran to the crest of the hill and stopped. All was wide and white in the moonlight and nowhere, anywhere, was there a sign.

And then, faint and far off, quickly stifled, a cry.

Faint ... lost, until he almost doubted his senses, but the cry of a woman, a cry for help.

Heedless of obstruction or ambush, he plunged down the trail. He darted around turns in the path until he had covered at least a hundred yards, then he slowed to listen.

No sound ... but there would not be. This was not a white man for no white man could have stolen a woman in such a way without noise. It had been an Apache ... or more likely, Apaches. Possibly the three they had met upon the trail, for they knew where Jordan and Maria Cristina were going.

And being Apaches, they knew every trick, every device, and they were men trained to desert war from childhood, men who would kill, and kill swiftly, for this was their way of life.

Yet they had his woman ...

Suddenly, somewhere off in the desert, he heard a sudden rush of horses, a pound of retreating hoofs.

He did not stop to swear or even to listen. Immediately he turned and ran back to the pool. Once there, he saddled the red horse and loaded his gear. It needed only a minute to roll her bed also and to fill the canteens. And then he was riding.

This much time he had taken, for upon an Apache trail there was no guessing how far a man would travel until he came up with them. Yet come up with them he would.

When he reached the place where the Indians had left their horses there was still a smell of dust in the air. The earth showed no tracks in the dim light and he dared not strike a match, yet he circled until he caught again the smell of dust and then started after them.

At any moment they might try an ambush, yet he had doubts of that for they were a small party, three or four at most. Twice, when well started, he got down to examine the ground. Here the earth was less torn and he could find the hoofprints. He pushed on until the moon was gone and the risk of losing the trail was too great.

Dismounting, he picketed the horse and settled down to wait. He rolled an endless chain of cigarettes and smoked until only half a sack of tobacco remained of his store. The last hour before dawn was endless, yet he waited and when the day became gray and the air was cold with morning he could see the tracks. Four horses, all unshod. One carried double.

Big Red was rested and eager. He lunged into the trail with that swift space-eating stride that was only his. And the miles fell behind with the trail's dust and the sun came up, hot and red. The desert turned to flame and sweat streaked the dust on Big Red's flanks and soaked Jordan's shirt. Twice he dismounted and walked, leading the horse to give him rest.

The trail led on and he forgot in the heat of the day's red sun the men who might be following him and thought only of the men ahead and of the girl they had.

And the tracks grew fresher. He was gaining. The gain was slight but nevertheless he gained.

It was hot ... no air stirred. He rode through a land that looked like Hell with the fires out, a land of great clinkers, burned out, destroyed ... a land of great serrated rocky spines, of tall spires and broken battlements, a land of deep canyons and washes where rain sometimes created streams, white now, and dead. Forests of yucca and armies of prickly pear, occasional elephant trees and clustered columns of the organ-pipe cactus.

It was a land unpeopled and still ... a gila monster moved upon a rock, a chaparral cock darted ahead of him. Yet the desert riders pushed on into the wasteland where the sun was a ball of fire in a sky of molten flame above a red and scarred land where the only sound was the muffled beat of his own horse's hoofs, the creak of his own saddle-leather.

Down there ahead of him, somewhere in the desert, must be a rancheria.

He did not stop for food. He ate from the sack and pushed on. The big red horse labored now but seemed to understand his rider's urgency. And he was stronger than the small grass-fed Apaches' ponies and he was gaining.

Once he glanced back. And felt his throat tighten when he did. Behind him was a plume of dust.

They had wasted no time in picking up his trail once he began moving. And there was no time for playing hare to their hounds now, no time for subterfuge. Now he must ride, ride, ride!

Then, far ahead, he saw dust. A wisp of dust, soon vanished. He broke into the open and saw them ahead of him. Three horses, hard-running. Three ... ?

Only just in time, he swung his horse. The realization that only three riders rode ahead caused its instant reaction. He swung the horse and a bullet whipped by his skull, missing by inches only. And then he saw the Apache streaking for his horse. With one hand he swung his Winchester and fired a shot.

The bullet spat dust just ahead of the fleeing

man and, slamming Big Red with the spurs, Jordan
went after him, working the lever on the Winchester as he rode.

The Apache despaired of reaching his horse and,
turning, fired. He shot too quick and missed and
then the big red horse slammed into him, hitting
him with a shoulder and knocking the Indian rolling.

Without slowing, Jordan went on, only taking
time to start the Apache's pony running.

The Apaches ahead spread out, taking different
directions. They must know of the men behind him
or they would have stopped to fight; but now they
ran. One man carried double and Jordan went
after him. Yet as he rode, he wondered ... would
they kill her when he reached them?

Suddenly Maria Cristina was fighting and then
with the pony at a dead run she twisted free and
flung herself from the saddle. She hit the sand,
bounding like a sack of old clothes, then rolling
over.

The Apache veered to pursue her and Jordan
came between them. The Apache swung his rifle
but Jordan parried the blow and struck up with
the butt. He knocked the rifle from the Indian's
hands and then they were off their horses and
fighting furiously.

The Apache's hand closed over his knife hilt just
as Jordan hit him with a long right. The blow
knocked him down and Jordan sprang for him with
both boots. The Indian rolled over and came up
fast and they closed, struggling fiercely. Then Jordan broke a hand free and struck upward with his

fist. The blow knocked the Indian back and Jordan kicked him in the knee with his boot heel.

The Apache was blocky, powerfully muscled and tough. He went down but rolled over and palmed his knife for a throw ... and Trace Jordan shot him through the body.

The Apache fell, tried to get up, then sprawled out. He lay still then, a slim brown body in the hot white sun, and the dust of the fighting sifted over him.

Trace Jordan mopped the sweat from his brow. Of the other Indians there was no sign. He turned slowly and walked toward Maria Cristina.

She was on her feet, facing him. Her face was dusty and her hair blew in the wind. It blew across her cheek. Her hands were bound together and her blouse was torn but she stood, feet apart, waiting for him.

He cut free her hands. For an instant they stood together, their eyes holding. He started to take her in his arms but she stepped back quickly, shrinking, her eyes wide like those of a frightened animal. "No! ... No! ..."

He let his hands fall. Turning, he went to where his horse waited and gathered up the reins. Then he rounded up an Apache pony and led it to her. Without comment she mounted and as she got into the Indian's blanket saddle he noticed she had taken the Indian's Winchester and ammunition. The cartridge belt was slung across her shoulder.

Behind them the dust was closer. He even believed he could distinguish figures through the dust.

They started, but not too fast. The horses behind them had come far and would be in no shape for a sprint. And his own horse needed rest.

They were riding north now and his thoughts were going on ahead. This was still Mexico but the Arizona border was north of them and they would reach the border sixty or seventy miles west of the Sutton-Bayless holdings. If they could reach a town, just any town where there was a sheriff....

But there was no town. Not close enough to help. Tubac was still farther west, Tucson and Tombstone too far north. Their best chance was the John Slaughter ranch at San Bernardino Springs. And there was a chance they could reach it in time. They might then claim sanctuary from John Slaughter and he was no man with whom to trifle, not even the Sutton outfit.

He led the way into an arroyo, then doubled back along the canyon to another, then out of it and into a thick forest of yucca and nopal. He used every trick now, riding slower, taking their time, their horses a dozen yards apart to raise less dust. They used the brush for cover, moving together, then apart.

Behind them the riders had separated, they had spread out to cover more ground. And they were gaining.

Suddenly he had an idea. It came to him out of nowhere, so foolish, so risky, so dangerous that for a moment he doubted his sanity. It was the fact that they were riding spread out that gave them a chance.

He glanced right and left, seeing some fairly

thick brush. Lifting a hand for a halt during the few minutes they were out of sight, he slid quickly to the ground and threw his horse. By the time Maria Cristina had come up, he had blindfolded his horse and, seeing what he had done, she slid to the ground and did likewise. Hurriedly then they gathered brush to cover both horses. Then they lay down under the edge of the brush themselves. Big Red was trembling but at the calming voices of Jordan and Maria Cristina both horses quieted, frightened by this sudden darkness in which they found themselves.

It was an old trick. Many a time he had seen horses led across rickety bridges in this way or taken from fires. A blindfolded horse lies quiet.

It was very hot. The heat of the earth was frightful. If one of the horses moved at the wrong time ... but the sudden darkness held them still.

Dust was thick beneath them. Gun in hand, he waited. Sweat ran down his face and he knew that if one of the riders swung closer and came into this space their concealment would not be sufficient. There was the smell of the horse, of his own unwashed clothing, and the mingled smells of creosote and crushed thamnosma. And then he heard the horses coming.

He heard two of them at once and was immediately sure they were too close. He tensed, ready to spring up shooting. If they got him he figured he could take at least two with him. He would ... he could hear a horse walking. He put a quieting hand on Big Red.

A man swore bitterly and he heard brush scrape

along his chaps. The man nearest them yelled, "See anything?"

"No!" The reply was from some distance off to the other side. "Canyon up ahead."

Their concealment was far from adequate. Only their pursuers were not expecting this and their eyes were looking ahead, always ahead.

The riders went by and then as he was about to look, another rider, and closer still. They heard the horse walking, heard a cork pulled from a canteen and the gurgle of water as the rider drank. At the moment he passed them he was plainly within view, only his head was tipped back and he was drinking. Then they heard him rinse his mouth and spit.

Trace Jordan lay still, counting a slow fifty. When he did take a chance and look he could see but one rider, some distance off. The rest must have gone down into the canyon the rider had mentioned. Swiftly they got to their feet and, ripping off the blindfolds, got the horses to their feet.

Turning at right angles they headed west, then turned north again, wanting to lose no miles that would carry them closer to safety. Soon they went into the forest of yucca, and when well inside were out of sight of anyone behind them.

What they had gained was at best a breathing spell. When Lantz found no more tracks he would begin searching. They would back-trail until they found the brush and the marks of the bodies. Jordan grinned, picturing the old tracker's disgust. But they had gained an hour, perhaps less.

Several intermittent streams that flowed only

during the rains lay between themselves and the border. Some of these flowed into the Rio de San Bernardino, and others to the Rio de Bavispe. The canyon of one of these streams might offer some protection for their ride to the border, although most of them ran northeast instead of northwest.

There was no run left in the Apache pony and little enough in the big red horse. And then they found the canyon they needed and, descending into it, they rode into the shallow water which flowed much of the distance over shelves of stone and they rode upstream.

For over a mile they rode in water scarcely hock-deep, then down to a thin sheet scarcely more than two inches in depth. They dismounted now and walked, liking the feeling of the cool water on their feet, leaving slow miles behind them and little trail.

Ten miles from the point at which they entered the canyon, they saw a way out and accepted the chance. Carefully they mounted the wall. At the rim, Jordan stepped down from the saddle and took a long, slow study of the country.

Wherever he looked the country was wide and barren. There were rocks and much cacti, thickets of mesquite, broken ledges upthrust from below.

Emerging, they proceeded with care. Exhaustion had drawn his face into haggard lines. Dust lay along the creases in his face. His eyeballs grated in their sockets and he rode in a daze of weariness. Half a length back, slumping in the saddle, Maria Cristina sat a horse that was all but ready to drop.

They needed rest, food and a chance to recuperate. They needed fodder for the horses.

When he first saw the scraggly-looking brush he was not impressed. It was like fifty other such vague clumps they had passed. It stretched out over most of an acre but what caught his attention was a dip in the ground at one edge of the clump. He rode nearer. It was a hollow nestled with brush and, inside, a small clearing. It was a doubtful-looking place but it offered shelter of an unsuspected kind. In the bottom of the hollow there was a small seep.

They could risk no fire but there was grass for the horses and water they could suck from the grass of the seep. Trace Jordan unsaddled the horses and put them on picket ropes, then began making a small pool by pulling clumps of grass in the wettest part of the seep. Maria Cristina returned to the clearing with some green leaves with reddish stems. These she soaked in water and held against a cut on her arm.

"Yerba mansa," Jordan said, looking at the leaves.

She looked up, faintly amused. "Well! What d'you know! You know the herbs."

"Some."

"Maybe you do well on your ranch. Maybe you good for something after all."

He chuckled. "You're hard to convince," he said. "I never saw a woman like you."

"What woman? I think you never see a woman. I think all you know is horse. Horse and fight." She looked at him critically. "You fight pretty good."

They divided the little jerky that was left and two somewhat battered sandy tortillas. They sat down together, watching the horses browse in the little circle of brush.

"You slow," she said. "What keep you today! I think maybe those Apaches get away with me."

There was the suspicion of a smile at the corners of her eyes and mouth. Deep within him something warm grew and mounted.

What a woman! To have a smile left after this! But it was there ... a little grim but no longer sullen. She reacted to the danger, the hardship and the flight with a wry smile and a touch of humor.

"Wasn't anxious to catch up," he said. "Soon's they found out what they had, they'd have got rid of you. Saved me some trouble."

"Hah? You think I'm no good for something?"

He looked at her, coolly estimating. "I think you're good for plenty," he said. "Sometime I'll show you some of the things you're good for."

She laughed outright, her eyes sparkling, taunting. "You think so? Me, I don' think so. I don' think you ever make it!"

CHAPTER FIVE

A fire was out of the question. They had lost their pursuit for the time being but even in this secluded place it would be foolish to risk the slightest smoke. Nor had they any food remaining but coffee and little of that.

Maria Cristina walked to the edge of the brush and watched the desert. The momentary lightness of her mood was gone. She was too wise in the ways of the country not to be completely aware of their situation. They had not won to freedom, only temporary delay. Ben Hindeman would discover at any time what they had done and once more would be on their trail.

Each hour of delay was a victory, yet each hour brought them closer to the final decision.

Had Maria Cristina not been with him Trace Jordan would have stopped running. Tired as he was, weak as he still was from his wound, he was nevertheless on the mend. Not even the grueling ride across the desert could keep his strength from rebuilding. Such life had now been his for a good many years.

If she had not been with him he would have turned back and begun to hunt the hunters. He would have been carrying the war to them, rather than running and hiding. Yet he must think of Maria Cristina first.

They were fortunate in their hiding place. There was enough grass and water for the horses and there would be enough to fill their canteens when they left. Also, it was not at all a likely place for any searchers to look. From the outside desert it seemed to offer nothing.

"Better get some sleep," he advised when she returned from the edge of the brush. "I'll keep watch."

"You sleep ... I watch." She looked at him with level eyes, aloof, remote once more. "I call you."

He was dead tired but he hesitated. Yet she was obviously wide awake and apparently in no mood for sleep. He walked to his bed roll and stretched out and almost at once his muscles let go and he sagged into sleep. The last thing he remembered was a little gust of wind stirring the leaves.

A hand on his shoulder awakened him to pitch darkness. He sat up, realizing there were no stars. The night was wild with wind and heavily overcast. The brush whipped hard and the horses stood with their backs to the wind, obviously uneasy.

"I see nothing. I rest now."

"All right." He pulled on his boots, got up and stamped his feet into them. "Feels like a storm."

"*Si* ... I think so."

Blown sand stung his cheek and he pulled his hat low to keep it on his head. Reaching for his gun belts, he slung them about his hips.

She moved past him in the darkness and he put his arm out and pulled her to him. Swiftly she struck down his hand and started to move away but, seized by a sudden hot gust of desire, he caught her and drew her into his arms.

She fought desperately, wickedly. Her body was suddenly a bunch of steel wire. She drew back, struggling to free herself. He caught her face and twisted her lips roughly toward him.

Distant lightning flashed and he saw her eyes were wide, her lips parted. He bent his head toward her and suddenly she caught the hair on the back of his head with both hands and crushed her mouth against his with fierce intensity. Her slim splendid body shaped itself against his and her lips parted . . . then suddenly she tore at his hands and jerked free, slapping him wickedly across the face. She sprang back then, like a cornered cat, standing against the brush, half-crouched.

"Don' touch me! Don' come near me! I *kill* you!"

For an instant he felt like taking her back into his arms and keeping her there whether she liked it or not but he let his hands fall. What she had said was no wild statement. If he tried to force himself on her she would kill him if she could.

"Have it your way." He picked up his rifle and started through the brush, then stopped and, grinning in spite of himself, he said, "But I'll always remember you liked it . . . for a minute, anyway."

"You are animal . . . I think I hate you."

"You're animal too," he said, chuckling, "and I like it that way."

"You think I am cheap woman."

"I don't think anything of the kind. I think you're a mighty fine woman but you're balky as a mustang."

"You are a fool."

The night was black and wild. Distant lightning weirdly lit the desert, turning into a pale moonscape this ash heap from the world's creation. Thunder rumbled and muttered in the far-off canyons, giant boulders seeming to tumble down vast corridors of stone. The wind skittered leaves along the ground and whipped the brush with savage gusts.

Near the edge of the brush he sat down. There not even the lightning would reveal his presence.

The wind was rising ... branches flew along the sand and tiny particles stung his face. The wind cuffed and slapped him, thrusting hard against his shoulder. If it became worse there would be no reason to remain longer for the horses were not resting and it was doubtful if Maria Cristina would sleep.

It was raining in the mountains and soon the washes would be running bank-full, wild torrents of water rushing down from the barren slopes of the mountains to turn their dry beds into raging rivers for a few short hours. The canyons would be running twenty feet deep in roaring water soon ...

A spatter of rain fell ... then another. He went to his saddle for his slicker and from Maria Cristina's saddle he got her poncho and spread it over her.

At the moment he spread it over her the lightning flashed.

She was apparently sleeping soundly, her face in repose, lovely as a madonna. All the fierce anger, the sudden aloofness, all that was gone.

He reached down and touched her hair. So black ... so very black. Like midnight caught in a web. For a moment he held a strand in his fingers, then replaced it gently and got to his feet. He took up his rifle and started back to his place at the edge of the brush and he did not see her hand come up and touch the strand of hair he had caressed. Nor did he see her eyes, wide open in the darkness.

There were scattered dashes of rain and gusts of wind. He watched the lightning-lit desert for an hour and then another. And then it was suddenly colder and in a lightning flash he saw a solid wall of rain advancing across the desert. Swiftly he came to his feet and turned toward the camp.

Maria Cristina was up, rolling her bed. She glanced around at him, her words torn by the wind. "We go, yes?"

"Better ... horses might stampede. Anyway, we can't rest and they won't."

He saddled up in a driving, pelting rain. Both got onto their horses and started north. Rain hammered their backs in savage gusts and the horses moved out fast, glad to be moving ahead of the storm and away from the whipping brush.

All night they drifted before the storm. Twice they crossed deep washes only minutes before rolling walls of water swept down and once lightning struck so near they smelled the sharp odor of sulphur in the air and their scalps prickled with electricity.

Suddenly, ahead of them, they heard a vast roar. Then they saw a canyon running with a tremendous rush of water. There was no question of getting through. No question at all. That water might be ten feet deep or forty feet and no horse living could swim in that mighty torrent.

Lightning flashed and Trace Jordan caught Maria Cristina's shoulder, gesturing toward some rocks. They rode toward it and found an overhang with its back to the storm.

Once under the rock they were out of the rain and away from the wind. He swung down and lifted her from the horse. Then he led the two horses deeper into the cavernlike overhang and tied them to a limb of cedar that stretched into the gloom.

Rain swept by the opening and the wind was cold. He glanced at Maria Cristina and she was shivering. Her legs from the knees down were wet.

Heedless of risk, he gathered dry sticks and built a fire. The horses were restless and frightened by the storm but a fire would calm them. Most horses accustomed to campfires enjoy their presence and all night long will feed closer and then away from the fire, liking its friendliness and assurance of companionship.

There was a pack rat's nest that offered a liberal supply of dry wood and by now it was close to dawn. There would be no light this morning until late for the sky was heavily overcast still and there was no evidence of a break.

How far they had come he had no idea but the storm would have wiped out their trail completely. There was a very good chance they were free at last. Not even Lantz could find tracks where there were none.

With daylight he should recognize this country. Now they were again in an area with which he was familiar. North of them, not too far away now, was the San Bernardino Ranch and he had visited the place, had covered all that country north to Tucson and even to Prescott and Congress.

Shivering, they huddled near the fire. The big red horse stamped and there was a momentary lull in the storm.

"Tomorrow we will be safe. I know the man on this ranch. He is a hard man but a good man."

"I hope."

"He is ... his name is Slaughter."

"He has kill men."

"Yes ... when they needed it." He added fuel to the fire. "So have I."

"Before this?"

"Yes."

"How many?"

"Four ... five, maybe."

They waited out a blast of wind. Some rain whipped into the overhang and the fire hissed and spluttered.

"You never tell me: Why you kill Bob Sutton?"

Taking his time, he explained about Johnny Hendrix and the horses. He told her of working through stampede and storm, through the dust of long cattle drives and the smell of burning hair around branding fires. And then of their months of effort to catch, brand and tame the horses, of this struggle to become something more than mere cowhands, to begin a business of their own. Then he told of his return from Durango and of finding the body of his friend.

"Jack Sutton," she said, "that was like him. And Mort Bayless, I think. He is another."

Trace Jordan went to the pack rat's nest for fuel. He dropped an armful near the fire and then walked around the fire to sit down. But he stopped there, looking out into the morning.

Without their being aware of it the sky had grown lighter. Outside the overhang the brush and trees bent stark and black before driving sheets of rain. Water stood on the desert in scattered pools that reflected the vague light, pools like mirrors of steel under the lowering sky, gray and black with rain-weighted clouds.

All this Jordan saw. All that and something more. He saw also five rain-wet horses and five mounted men and all those men had rifles and all of them were looking at him.

So ... this far they had come and this close—and all for nothing at all.

He stood very still, yet his mind reached swiftly forward. As at all such times the minute seems to stand still in which each detail is impressed upon the mind.

He recognized the blocky man with the hard square face who would be Ben Hindeman. The narrow features of old Jacob Lantz and there were others whom he had never known and probably would never know. He saw their horses and three of those horses had belonged to him.

He saw them and he saw their guns and knew the chase was over. He knew that his raincoat was open, that his guns were at his thighs, that he could kill one, two or even three men before they got him.

It could be done. It had been done. Mysterious Dave Mathers had killed five men in a gun battle in Dodge; Commodore Perry Owen had shot down four in Holbrook.

But Maria Cristina sat by the fire close to him and she might be hit or she would be left to the vengeance of those who did not fall.

"Howdy, boys," he spoke casually. "Kind of wet out there, ain't it?"

At his voice, Maria Cristina looked up. Her face stiffened with shock and she got to her knees.

The heavy man in the slicker studied Jordan through the rain. It was no wonder, Hindeman thought, that it had taken so long. Lantz was right, this man was a curly wolf . . . with his back to the wall.

Jacob Lantz sat a little apart. He sat his saddle, looking at Jordan.

"You killed Old Bob?" Hindeman made a statement, rather than asked a question.

"He went for his gun."

"But you killed him . . . why?"

"You know why. He was riding a stolen horse. Stolen from me." He nodded his head to indicate their own horses. "That steeldust is mine, so's the sorrel. And that dun answers to the name of Pet."

He looked at the horse. "Pet!" he spoke sharply. The dun's head came up, ears pricked.

The riders sat silent. Hindeman was unmoved but Joe Sutton had a guilty feeling. No question about it, these horses had been stolen and from this man. The feeling touched them all and made them uneasy, less sure of their ground.

"Makes no difference now," Hindeman said. "We're goin' to hang you."

"Don't say 'we' . . . there's three, maybe four of you aren't goin' to hang me. Maybe none of you will. Wait until the shootin's over . . . plenty of time to talk about hangin'."

Ben Hindeman studied the man and Ben was no fool. They were five to one . . . unless the girl declared herself in and it was likely she would. She had been quick enough to take a shot at Jack, that day.

Five to one. They had their rifle muzzles down, for the discovery of the hiding place had been sheer accident. They had only to lift their rifles but this man had only to draw; and Ben Hindeman knew any man who could beat Old Bob on an even break and who could outguess Jack Sutton would be fast and sure.

No question about it, somebody was going to die if shooting started.

"You throw down your guns," he said, "then the girl won't get hurt."

"*No!*"

Maria Cristina's voice laid across the morning like a whip. "Do not do it! They will only kill you! If you put down the guns, *I* will shoot!"

Ben Hindeman sat stolidly on his horse in the hard falling rain. For the first time in his life he was utterly at a stalemate.

Maria Cristina would shoot and she had a rifle. They might kill her but Ben Hindeman could not see a woman killed. Not like this.

He looked from the woman to the man, this lean fierce unbeatable man, his face haggard and unshaved, his back to the wall . . . but ready.

And this woman who stood now, her feet apart, her body poised to move, her eyes wide and beautiful but dangerous.

He knew with a kind of sickness that men would die here and a woman. And that never again would he ever look any man in the face without shame if she were killed. He looked at Jordan and for a long minute their eyes held and Hindeman knew with a sense of failure that there was no way out.

Nor did he have any false heroics about him. He was under no necessity to prove his courage and dying here today would prove nothing.

This was not the way he had planned it. To ride a man down, to trap him, to kill him in a blaze of gunfire. That was another thing.

But here was a showdown and Ben Hindeman was a man who knew how to retreat.

"Mind if we come in out of the rain?" he asked mildly.

There was no other word spoken for a long minute and in that minute Jacob Lantz started to walk his horse. He started slow but he was walking away. Whatever he had seen, the others had not.

He was getting out of the line of fire. And he had promised he would do just that.

"No, by God!"

Across the stillness of the morning Mort Bayless' voice lashed like a bull whip. And as he spoke, he grabbed for his gun.

Of them all, he alone did not have a rifle in his hand and it was he who chose to open the ball. He recognized, in Ben Hindeman's quiet question, a yielding and his hand struck down for the gun.

Trace Jordan saw it all, saw it clearly and sharply. The black figures of the men etched against the slate-gray sky of morning, the driving rain, the horses darkened by rain, the ground steel-gray and glistening. He caught the essence of the moment in that instant, that flickering fragment of time when Mort Bayless' drive to kill pushed them over the brink they sought to avoid.

Mort grabbed wildly. His hand caught his gun butt and the edge of his slicker. In any event, he would not have made it in time. A bullet smashed him through the body and as he slid from the saddle and his horse sprang from under him, a second bullet drilled a neat blue hole in his skull.

And then for a brief moment the lightning of the guns replaced the lightning of the storm and the stillness following the thunder was filled by the hard sharp reports of the guns.

In the split second after Mort's voice, Jordan thought Hindeman gave a sort of groan and Jordan knew a sort of sympathy for a man saddled with such companions.

A moment—and it was over, a moment of brutal

134

smashing gunfire. Mort, knocked from his horse, hit the ground in a pool of water. The man behind him, knocked off balance, was momentarily out of action.

Trace Jordan had fired at Mort Bayless and then threw himself aside and took a quick shot at Ben Hindeman, knowing he was the toughest and most dangerous man. Hindeman took the bullet and was knocked lopsided in the saddle, his gun going off into the ground.

From the ground near him Jordan heard the wicked blast of the Winchester '73. He felt a bullet from somewhere tear at his shoulder and steadied himself for another shot at Hindeman. The man knocked off balance by Bayless' fall was lying still. Jordan fired again and then threw himself away from the girl to draw fire from her. She shot from the ground again and then a bullet from Hindeman spat rock into his face and he shot the big man a second time.

A man on a lunging horse swung the horse around and lifted his gun to chop a shot. Jordan and Maria Cristina fired at the same instant and the man threw up his hands.

The horse broke into a plunging run and the rider stayed with him for six or seven jumps, then spilled off, arms and legs thrown wide to hit with a splash of water like a doll thrown carelessly. The man lay sprawled and wet and dead.

So quickly it happened, so quickly it was over. A moment of madness laced by gunfire, a moment of thundering guns and spitting lead, and then only the quiet and the rain falling.

Slowly he straightened up. He held both guns, never conscious that he had drawn the second. Shoving one into his holster, he began to reload. One gun was empty, the other held but two shells. And he had no memory of firing more than three, perhaps four times.

Maria Cristina got up from the rock where she had knelt, half-concealed by boulders and brush.

"You are hurt?" she asked.

"A scratch."

He stood there a minute or two, looking out into the rain. Jacob Lantz was still around and, although the tracker had left before the shooting started, he might declare himself in at long range. And he had the reputation of being good with a rifle.

Trace Jordan walked out into the rain. Lantz was nowhere in sight.

Mort Bayless stared up into the sodden clouds, his eyes wide to the sky, unheeding the pounding rain. Blood stained the pool in which he lay. His shirt was plastered to his thin body, all the evil in him a thing gone now, emptied out of him with his life.

Ben Hindeman was lying there too but he was not dead.

He had been hit three times, once by the rifle. He made a feeble futile grasp toward his fallen gun and then lay quiet, looking up at Jordan.

"Is it bad?"

Trace looked at him. One bullet through his left side but low down. Another through his chest but high enough to have missed the lung. The third through his thigh.

"You're hit," Jordan said. "Can be bad."

"I got a wife," Hindeman said. "A good woman. A man should think of those things."

He closed his eyes momentarily, then opened them. "They never should have stolen those horses," he said. "The damn' fools."

Another man lay beyond Hindeman, sprawled out, one knee buckled under him. The fourth man, the one knocked down by Bayless' horse, still lay where he had dropped. There was no blood on him.

Trace Jordan holstered his gun and stooped to pick up Ben Hindeman. As he stooped he heard the click of a drawn-back hammer and turned quickly.

Jacob Lantz stood there with empty hands held wide from his body. Maria Cristina had covered him with a Winchester.

"Help you with that?" Lantz asked. "He's a heavy man."

Together they carried him under the overhang and after one careful searching look at Lantz, Maria Cristina put her rifle down. "Make a fire," she told him.

Then she turned to Jordan. "You first," she said.

"He's hard hit," Trace said. "I can wait."

Maria Cristina shrugged. "Suppose he dies? He would have killed you."

"Him first," Jordan told her flatly. "Get busy."

She looked at him, their eyes holding on each other. Then she knelt beside Hindeman. "You think you strong," she said, glancing up. "I think you big fool."

Hindeman chuckled, then gasped at the pain. But he looked up at Jordan. "I think you've got you a woman, Friend."

He looked past Trace Jordan at Lantz. "What happened to you?" he asked hoarsely.

Lantz bared his broken teeth in a grin. "I told you ... I'd trail him. I wouldn't fight him. When I seen what Mort was fixin' to do, I taken out."

Jordan glanced out to where the other men lay. The man who had been knocked down by Bayless was gone. He had evidently lain quiet until the shooting was over and at the first chance, ducked out. Some were like that. Sometimes the ones who swaggered the most. Like Ike Clanton at the O.K. Corral fight.

Maria Cristina bathed the wounds in a decoction made of a desert plant, than bandaged them as best she could. From the plant named *sangre de Cristo* she had taken the sap, which coagulates quickly, to stop the blood from the wounds.

By the time the wounds were cared for and Lantz had buried the dead men, it was midday. He came back inside. "Rain's breakin'," he said. "Better get set for trouble."

"Trouble?"

"Yeah," Lantz took his time. "There's one got away, an' more comin'. If that one's lucky, he'll fetch up with those who been comin' behind us. You can just bet they'll come huntin' you."

Ben Hindeman spoke from his pallet. "The fight's over, Jake. You tell 'em I said so. We're through."

"Buck might listen. Wes Parker won't. Some of the others might not, either."

"Then you light out an' stop 'em," Hindeman said harshly. He lifted himself to an elbow. "Stop 'em an' get a buckboard down here for me. If you can't stop 'em, ride like hell for John Slaughter's outfit."

The clouds broke and the rain drifted away. The sun returned and the pools began to disappear. Only the greener vegetation and the dampness around the rocks remained to remind them of the storm.

Trace Jordan took his rifle and led the horses to a patch of grass where they could be picketed in plain sight of the shelter. He was far less worried by the Sutton-Bayless riders than by the Apaches. For several days now both the pursuers and the pursued had been leaving tracks all over this corner of Sonora, an area that was Apache country.

Any hunter from one of the rancherias might have come upon those tracks, or any squaw out gathering herbs or firewood could have seen them. In a country where a white man could scarcely turn over in bed without an Apache knowing it, it was absurd to believe they would not be aware of all that had happened.

Moreover, the Apaches who escaped from the kidnapping of Maria Cristina must by now be seeking them out. Yet wherever he looked, the desert was empty.

Returning to the overhang, he found Maria Cristina sitting by the rocks with a rifle at hand. Their eyes met and no words were needed. Both had grown up in Indian country; they understood the gravity of their situation.

They were two people with a wounded man on their hands and no telling when help would reach them. The rain had wiped out their trail, yet the Apaches well knew where they would be going. It was only a matter of time until they were discovered.

They now had four horses picketed and Jordan considered rigging a litter between two of them, yet these horses were unused to any such contrivance and would be frightened by it. They were, at best, just broken to the saddle.

Slowly the hours dragged by and there was nothing. The danger grew greater by the minute and Jordan was restless and irritable.

Ben Hindeman began to mutter and complain. His fever mounted and he became delirious. Maria Cristina sat with him, keeping damp cloths on his head. Several times she mixed concoctions used by the Indians for fever and they helped; but Hindeman had lost blood from his wounds and his condition was far from good.

Raiding parties from the Sierra Madre used this route and the Chiricahuas had their stronghold in the mountains just north of the border.

By noon of the second day Jordan knew something must be done. He had been leaning on the rocks staring into the desert's heat waves when he made his decision. With some poles and two ponchos he rigged a litter between two horses. With Maria Cristina's help, Hindeman was loaded into the litter and, holding the horses to a walk, they made their start.

It was slow going ... yet by dusk they had covered fifteen miles and camped in a cluster of rocks near an intermittent stream.

Ben Hindeman's face was flushed and he looked bad. Jordan stared down at the wounded man, considering the irony of the situation. Only hours ago this man had been hunting him to kill and now he, Jordan, was trying to save the man from death by bullets he had himself fired! And risking his own life to do it.

Rifle in hand, Trace Jordan walked out from camp. The illness from his own wounds had cut down his weight. He was lean and raw-boned, even tougher-looking than usual and his clothing was battered and worn from days and nights of travel.

Yet the years of wilderness living had conditioned him to a hard life and ... he had gone only a few yards when he saw the tracks. The tracks of a man walking.

A wounded man ... a white man.

The man had staggered as he walked. Once he had gone to his knees. Absorbed in the trail, Trace Jordan followed it along for a half-mile. Twice the man had fallen in that distance. At the second place there was blood on the desert.

Jordan went up to some rocks and from the slight vantage point they gave him, began a minute examination of the terrain. Suddenly, some distance north, he saw a dark object on the desert.

It might be a rock. But there was a subtle difference that told him it was not. He started north, walking fast.

Even before he reached the body he knew who it was. Old Jacob Lantz had led many a foray against the Apache but he had led his last one. He lay sprawled in the desert and he was dead. But his body was neither cold nor stiff.

He had been shot three times but one of the wounds was at least a day old. Evidently on the first day out from the overhang, Lantz had been wounded and his horse killed. By some artifice he had evaded the Apache and started on . . . on foot.

Today, probably within the last few hours, they had come up with him again. And if they had killed him no longer ago than that, they must be close by. They might have found the tracks of the four horses coming north.

Hurriedly he turned and made his way back to the rocks. As he walked, he made plans. Despite their weariness and Ben Hindeman's condition they must move on tonight. Rarely would Apaches attack at night and they preferred not even to travel at night. The border could not be more than fifteen to twenty miles away and the border was where lay the ranch at San Bernardino Springs.

Maria Cristina came swiftly to her feet when she saw his face and Jordan explained, holding back nothing at all.

Hindeman was conscious. "You two take out," he said. "Small chance I'll make it, anyway."

"You'll make it," Jordan told him dryly. "You're too mean to die."

As soon as it was dark they loaded up and just

before they rode off, Jordan built a fire and stacked fuel so it would fall into the flames. Due north then, holding a course on the polestar, they rode. The desert was broken and rough but they made good time.

"Keep goin'," Hindeman told them. "Don't pay me no mind. If them 'Paches get me it won't matter, anyway."

So they pushed on through the night and in the first gray of dawn, with the horses wearily plodding, they glimpsed far off a cluster of buildings.

At the same instant Maria Cristina called out, "Trace!"

He turned in the saddle. Behind them and to the east, not six hundred yards away, a dozen Indians sat their horses. They had come out of an arroyo and were apparently as surprised as Jordan himself.

"Keep moving," he told her. "Keep moving no matter what."

They rode on, holding their pace. Suddenly the Indians began to move out. Their ponies began to trot.

Trace Jordan stepped up the pace. The buildings were not more than five miles away now. The Indians were very close and coming up rapidly.

Turning, Trace Jordan, lifting his Winchester, took careful aim. He took up the slack on his trigger, took a deep breath, let part of it out, then took up more slack, then a little—the rifle leaped in his hands and a horse jumped and fell back, throwing his rider.

Twice more he fired; then, waiting to see the

effectiveness of his shots, he raced after Maria Cristina and the litter.

With shrill yells the Indians came after him. Suddenly, at the buildings, a rider appeared around the corner of a barn and started for them. Behind him came other riders until seven were strung out, racing their horses.

Trace heard shooting and, turning his horse, he emptied his rifle at some two hundred yards distance. An Indian on a paint pony fell from his horse and rolled over, got up, then fell again. Then a horse shied violently at another shot and the Indians slowed up and spread out.

Jordan ran his horse after the litter, feeding the shells into his rifle. When he looked back again the Indians had broken off their pursuit and turned away.

The riders from the ranch came up and swung their horses alongside. Their leader was a small square-shouldered man with cold gray eyes.

"Hindeman!" he said sharply. " 'Paches get you?"

"No." Ben Hindeman indicated Jordan. "He did."

On the second morning following their arrival at Rancho San Bernardino, Trace Jordan came out into the morning sunlight and pulled on his hat. It was very early and John Slaughter was still at breakfast. Ben Hindeman was sleeping and apparently much improved.

There had been no sign of the other riders from the Sutton-Bayless outfit.

Buck Bayless and Wes Parker had not been among those in the fight at the rocks and Hindeman would say nothing about them. Yet something in his manner made Jordan increasingly restless.

The Indian girl who helped in the kitchen was throwing out some water. She looked quickly at Trace Jordan and started for the house.

"Seen Maria Cristina?" he asked.

The girl looked at him curiously. She shook the last few drops from the pan. "She gone. She gone maybe two hours."

"*What?*"

"She take horse. She say goodby, all. She ride away."

"Where'd she go?" he demanded.

The girl shrugged. "Where? I don't know. She say nothing. Just go."

Swearing, Trace ran for the corral. He hastily threw a saddle on the big red horse and stepped into the leather. Without a backward glance, he started down the trail.

Maria Cristina would go home, of course. She had been obviously disturbed by the fact that nothing was known of Buck Bayless or Wes Parker. Bayless she knew and he did not worry her. Wes Parker was another of the crowd who ran with Jack Sutton and Mort and the more Jordan thought of it, the more reason he could see for her worry. Yet it was not that alone and he knew it.

Maria Cristina had carefully avoided being alone with him since their arrival at Slaughter's. She had evaded any chance of a private talk without seeming to do anything of the kind. Whatever she was thinking he did not know, but obviously she did not intend to share her thoughts with him.

Several times he had caught her looking at him, wide-eyed and serious, yet she always looked away and her manner had been cool.

The trail led through Guadalupe Pass and there was a chance he could overtake her there. He knew there was a spring in the Pass itself or near the opening of the Pass and there were several springs just north of the Pass at different points. Beyond the Guadalupes the country was unfamiliar to him except for that area covered in his flight.

He rode steadily into the morning and from time to time he saw her tracks. Six or seven miles from the Rancho she stopped at a tank to water her horse, then pushed on. She was holding a steady gait and he saw no other evidences of travel but those made by her pony.

Word was out that Apache raiding parties were riding, which was enough to stop all travel. It was no time for a lone man to be on the road, to say nothing of a pretty girl. Yet before he could even see the cleft that marked the Pass, he saw a rider on a bay horse coming toward him.

Trace Jordan slid the loop off his gun butt and eased himself in the saddle, holding his pace. The rider came on, a little slower.

When not more than two hundred yards separated them, Jordan slowed his horse. At the same moment he recognized the rider as the man who had warned him away after drinking with him in Tokewanna.

"Howdy." Jordan drew up.

The man's face was pale under the tan. "I'm Joe Sutton," he said, "and I'm not huntin' trouble."

"Then there will be no trouble."

Joe Sutton took the makings from his pocket and began to roll a smoke. "You ... did you see anything of Ben? And the others?"

"I saw them . . . Ben's at Slaughter's and he's alive. I think he'll pull through."

The match broke in Sutton's fingers and Jordan leaned over and held his cigarette to Sutton's.

"Mort?"

"He's dead ... so's Old Jake but the Apaches did that, not me."

He explained, taking his time, just what had happened at the rocks and after. He told of the ride back to the border with Ben Hindeman.

"Pass anybody on the trail?" he asked then.

"No." Sutton looked thoughtful. "Saw some tracks, though. They showed up just inside the Pass so whoever made 'em must have turned off."

"What happened to Buck Bayless and that fellow Parker?"

Joe Sutton shrugged. "Parker is dead ... Bayless is hurt but not bad. The way I hear it, they went to the North to try to make that Chavero kid tell where his sister went. They ran into Vicente."

"And ... ?"

"I reckon we had Vicente figured all wrong. He wasn't about to back down. So Buck says. Vicente told Wes to travel an' Wes didn't take to it. We buried Wes next morning."

There was still a thing to be settled. Jordan wanted to be riding on, but there was no time better than now. There had been too much killing and Joe Sutton seemed a reasonable man.

"Ben Hindeman said the fight's over. I'm getting my horses back."

"Ben's the boss." Joe Sutton was relieved. "Fool thing, anyhow." He threw down his cigarette, half-smoked. "Jack and Mort . . . yes, and Wes too. They got us into more trouble than we could get out of."

Trace Jordan reined his horse over. "See you," he said and put Big Red down the trail. Being a cautious man, he glanced back but Joe Sutton was riding on.

It was almost sundown when he found her. Maria Cristina had made camp in a little wooded draw off the Pass. She got up from the fire as he rode up, her face without expression. He swung his horse alongside the fire.

"What did you ride off for?" he demanded irritably.

"I do not run. I go home."

She knelt beside the fire, knelt suddenly as if her knees had weakened. She began fussing over the food she was preparing. In the late afternoon light her face seemed unnaturally pale.

He swung down. "Damn it, you didn't have to run off! You could have said something!"

"Why? Who I say something to? . . . To you?"

"I don't want you going off like that," he protested. "This is no time for a woman to be traveling alone."

She did not look up, adding sticks to the fire. Then she added sullenly, "I am all right."

The words he had been thinking on the trail were gone. Somewhere he had lost them. He told
148

her of Vicente and Wes Parker but she would not look at him. She put coffee in the water and got up.

He stepped around the fire and took her by the arms. "Maria Cristina, I don't want you going away. Not ever again. I want you with me."

She turned on him, looking up into his eyes, and there was no longer sullenness there, or anger. "You don't know what you say."

"I know all right."

She tried to draw away from him, her eyes suddenly wary, half-frightened. "No . . . you take your hands off." She tried, ineffectually, to twist out of his grip.

"Don't do that!" he said sharply, angrily. He drew her swiftly into his arms, her body coming against his. She looked up at him, her eyes very black and suddenly burning, almost hungry.

Then desperately, fiercely, she fought him. She fought to twist free, to get away. He held her, then slowly and inexorably he brought her mouth around to his.

She twisted her face away, fighting like a panther to escape, then suddenly, fiercely, she turned her mouth to his and their lips met and clung.

He held her, saying nothing. "Just ain't halter-broke," he said gently, "but you'll do. You'll do all right."

She stood quiet in his arms and the big red horse moved off a few steps and fell to cropping grass. He had his own degrees of patience and was becoming accustomed to the oddities of human behavior.

Later, when most of the coffee had boiled away, Jordan drank it, black and strong.

She looked at him, her eyes soft in the gathering dusk. "You know one time I say I don't think you ever make it?"

"I remember."

"Well . . . now I think maybe you make it."

She laughed then, a laugh teasing and tender, a soft laughter that lost itself with the campfire smoke in the brush along the canyon's wall.

ABOUT LOUIS L'AMOUR

"I think of myself in the oral tradition—as a troubadour, a village taleteller, the man in the shadows of the campfire. That's the way I'd like to be remembered—as a storyteller. A good storyteller."

It is doubtful that any author could be as at home in the world recreated in his novels as Louis Dearborn L'Amour. Not only could he physically fill the boots of the rugged characters he writes about, but he has literally "walked the land my characters walk." His personal experiences as well as his lifelong devotion to historical research have combined to give Mr. L'Amour the unique knowledge and understanding of the people, the events, and the challenge of the American frontier that have become the hallmarks of his popularity.

Of French-Irish descent, Mr. L'Amour can trace his own family in North America back to the early 1600s and follow their steady progression westward, "always on the frontier." As a boy growing up in Jamestown, North Dakota, he absorbed all he could about his family's frontier heritage, including the story of his great-grandfather who was scalped by Sioux warriors.

Spurred by an eager curiosity and desire to broaden his horizons, Mr. L'Amour left home at the age of fifteen and enjoyed a wide variety of jobs including seaman, lumberjack, elephant handler, skinner of dead cattle, assessment miner, and officer on tank destroyers during World War II. During his "yondering" days he also circled the world on a freighter, sailed a dhow on the Red Sea, was shipwrecked in the West Indies and stranded in the Mojave Desert. He has won fifty-one of fifty-nine fights as a professional boxer and worked as a journalist and lecturer. A voracious reader and collector of rare books, Mr. L'Amour's personal library of some 10,000 volumes covers a broad range of scholarly disciplines including many personal papers, maps, and diaries of the pioneers.

Mr. L'Amour "wanted to write almost from the time I could walk." After developing a widespread following for his many adventure stories written for the fiction magazines, Mr. L'Amour published his first full-length novel, *Hondo*, in 1953. Mr. L'Amour is now one of the four bestselling living novelists in the world. Every one of his more than 95 books are still in print and every one has sold more than one million copies. He has more million-copy bestsellers than any other living author. His books have been translated into more than a dozen languages, and more than thirty of his novels and stories have been made into feature films and television movies.

His hardcover bestsellers include *The Lonesome Gods; The Walking Drum*, his twelfth-century historical novel; *Jubal Sackett; Last of the Breed;* and *The Haunted Mesa*.

The recipient of many great honors and awards, in 1983 Mr. L'Amour became the first novelist ever to be awarded a Special National Gold Medal by the United States Congress in honor of his life's work. In 1984 he was also awarded the Medal of Freedom by President Ronald Reagan.

Mr. L'Amour lives in Los Angeles with his wife, Kathy, and their two children, Beau and Angelique.

BANTAM'S #1
ALL-TIME BESTSELLING AUTHOR
AMERICA'S FAVORITE FRONTIER WRITER

☐	25206	HELLER WITH A GUN	$2.95
☐	24550	BOWDRIE'S LAW	$2.95
☐	23368	BOWDRIE	$2.95
☐	25100	CROSS FIRE TRAIL	$2.95
☐	25402	SHOWDOWN AT YELLOW BUTTE	$2.95
☐	25580	CHANCY	$2.95
☐	26119	SITKA	$3.50
☐	27047	THE CHEROKEE TRAIL	$3.50
☐	25090	MOUNTAIN VALLEY WAR	$2.95
☐	25477	TAGGART	$2.95
☐	25972	HIGH LONESOME	$2.95
☐	25030	BORDEN CHANTRY	$2.95
☐	24957	BRIONNE	$2.95
☐	25303	THE FERGUSON RIFLE	$2.95
☐	25742	KILLOE	$2.95
☐	25770	CONAGHER	$2.95
☐	25973	NORTH TO THE RAILS	$2.95
☐	24906	THE MAN FROM SKIBBEREEN	$2.95
☐	24743	SILVER CANYON	$2.95
☐	24767	CATLOW	$2.95
☐	24765	GUNS OF THE TIMBERLANDS	$2.95
☐	24762	HANGING WOMAN CREEK	$2.95
☐	22636	FALLON	$2.50
☐	24760	UNDER THE SWEETWATER RIM	$2.95
☐	25221	MATAGORDA	$2.95
☐	25324	DARK CANYON	$2.95
☐	20956	THE CALIFORNIOS	$2.50

Prices and availability subject to change without notice.

BANTAM'S #1
ALL-TIME BESTSELLING AUTHOR
AMERICA'S FAVORITE FRONTIER WRITER

☐ 25673 **JUBAL SACKETT** **$3.95**

Be sure to read the rest of the titles in the Sackett series: follow them from the Tennessee mountains as they head west to ride the trails, pan the gold, work the ranches, and make the laws.

☐ 25271	SACKETT'S LAND	$2.95
☐ 25272	TO THE FAR BLUE MOUNTAIN	$2.95
☐ 25273	WARRIOR'S PATH	$2.95
☐ 25274	RIDE THE RIVER	$2.95
☐ 25275	THE DAY BREAKERS	$2.95
☐ 25276	SACKETT	$2.95
☐ 25504	LANDO	$2.95
☐ 25505	MOJAVE CROSSING	$2.95
☐ 25506	THE SACKETT BRAND	$2.95
☐ 25507	THE LONELY MEN	$2.95
☐ 24208	TREASURE MOUNTAIN	$2.95
☐ 25509	MUSTANG MAN	$2.95
☐ 24205	GALLOWAY	$2.95
☐ 25511	THE SKYLINERS	$2.95
☐ 24956	THE MAN FROM BROKEN HILLS	$2.95
☐ 24212	RIDE THE DARK TRAIL	$2.95
☐ 24203	LONELY ON THE MOUNTAIN	$2.95

BANTAM
SHOP-AT-HOME
C·A·T·A·L·O·G

Special Offer
Buy a Bantam Book
for only 50¢.

Now you can have Bantam's catalog filled with hundreds of titles plus take advantage of our unique and exciting bonus book offer. A special offer which gives you the opportunity to purchase a Bantam book for only 50¢. Here's how!

By ordering any five books at the regular price per order, you can also choose any other single book listed (up to a $5.95 value) for just 50¢. Some restrictions do apply, but for further details why not send for Bantam's catalog of titles today!

Just send us your name and address and we will send you a catalog!